DOUBTFUL BOUNTY

by

Stoney Livingston

Copyright 2015 by Stoney Livingston
All rights reserved
ISBN:0692399593
ISBN-13: 978-0692399590

Published by Chokonen Press
Tucson, Arizona
1st printing April, 2015

Chapter 1

Bill Rutelege stood impatiently at the Pima County Superior Court records counter. He tapped his fingers on the Formica top and glanced at the large clock on the wall to his left as the clerk photocopied the original bond and stamped it as a certified copy.

"Here you are, Bill," said the clerk, placing the document on the worn counter top. "That'll be ten dollars."

"Ten dollars? When did you guys increase the price?"

"About two months ago."

"Oh, yeah, I guess I've had a dry spell."

"Yeah, I was wondering if you gave it up for Lent or something."

"I tried, but I got hungry."

The clerk eyed the bond then looked up at Bill. "You must be real hungry. This guy's bond is only five thousand. You only get, like, ten percent for bringing him in, right?"

Bill sighed. "Yeah, most of the time. I wish I could say this guy was an exception, but he isn't." Bill handed the man a ten-dollar bill.

The clerk accepted the money and busied himself making out a receipt. "You figure this guy is still in town?"

"No, but the indemnitor on the bond offered to pay

my expenses if I go after him."

"Where you gotta go?"

Bill arched an eyebrow and said nothing.

"Well, good hunting," said the clerk as he pushed the receipt in Bill's direction.

"Thanks."

It was dark when Bill pulled his '57 T-Bird into the parking lot of the restaurant on the Orange Avenue exit in Chula Vista, California. But it wasn't as late as he wanted it to be. He had traveled the four hundred fourteen miles from Tucson in less than six-and-a-half hours. He shrugged, a half-smile curling his lips. Oh well. He still had a few last minute preparations to make. He could take care of those matters and still have time for a cup of coffee.

He parked in a dark corner of the parking lot and snapped his borrowed California license plate over the maroon and white plate issued by Arizona. His man would be leery of anything with Arizona plates. The T-Bird stood out like a sore thumb as it was. No sense putting a sign on the door announcing he was a bounty hunter from Arizona out to slap old Ernie back into jail. He strolled into the restaurant, already feeling the adrenaline building in his body.

He studied his map of the San Diego area as he sipped black coffee and smoked a cigarette. He perused the contents of the file folder: Ernest L. Garcia, FTA (dui, possession). He loved the way the bondsmen jotted down information and filled out the required forms -- that should be the real crime. Normally, Bill picked up a copy of the original case report to get the specifics; this time he had been in too big a hurry. *Possession of what? And how much? What were the circumstances? And why did he fail to appear?* Oh, well, his ignorance was his own fault for not getting a copy of the original case.

He took a drag from his smoke and studied a brown stain on the wall, wondering if he would ever see it again; wondering how it got there and why it hadn't been cleaned; wondering if he would ever see anything again. You never really knew. A man on the run was always potentially dangerous, no matter what his original crime. He remembered Hoffman, a private investigator who tried his hand at hunting bounty. He was pretty good at it for about two years -- then he got too cocky. Went into Mexico looking for a misdemeanor FTA last year and came back to the States in a pine box. Stupid.

Bill glanced at the photograph of his suspect. He looked mean and tough and ugly, but then again, everyone looked mean and tough and ugly in a mug shot. He studied the picture and suddenly felt sorry for Ernie. He didn't look all that smart. Probably never got out of elementary school. *Damn. If I have to do this from time to time, I'd at least like to have the guy look a little smarter. Make me feel like I was arresting a real badass or something, instead of some stupid, uneducated bum that never had much of a chance to start with.*

He wondered if he was checking the right lead first. Yeah, the ex-wife was his best bet. Several of Ernesto Garcia's friends had indicated he had returned to California. Yeah, he'd check the ex-wife first. If he struck out there, he'd follow up that lead on the San Diego phone number given to him by Ernesto's sister, though he thought that to be a waste of time. He'd checked out the number through a friend of his with a PI agency in Orange County and found it registered to a "D. Callahan" in San

Diego. Probably meant to throw him off.

Bill glanced at his watch and gulped down the remaining coffee. Almost nine p.m. If he had to do these kinds of jobs, he generally liked to do them about this time. It was still early enough that a roving police car wouldn't stop him as a suspicious person if he was walking the sidewalk in a residential area, yet it was late enough that if his man was not out on the town, he would be engrossed in some prime-time television show, or drinking, or shooting up, or he would be in bed -- asleep, or "playing house." If he were out, Bill would wait. That was even better than finding him at home. He could get him outside of the house when he came home.

Bill made one last glance at the map, then folded it and placed it in his briefcase. His reconnaissance of the house should take about five to ten minutes. Twelve to fifteen minutes to get there from here. Park the car on the main drag, about two blocks from the suspect residence. Load up with handcuffs, pistol, flashlight, knife and short-barreled shotgun, and walk to the house. Another four minutes. If Ernesto was there, he could measure his freedom at one minute less than the Bill Cosby Show -- starting *now*.

In the parking lot, Bill opened the trunk of his T-Bird. Everything he needed was laid out in a towel. He didn't need a light. He glanced about the parking lot and deftly picked up the towel and its contents and placed them on the seat of his car. As he sat behind the wheel and put his holstered Smith and Wesson .357 magnum onto his belt, his hands trembled. He could feel the uncertainty building in his body.

Damn! I can't stand this. I feel like a bigger

criminal than the guy I'm looking for. Why can't the cops find him and book him, instead of writin' me speeding tickets? They've got a helluva lot more resources than I do.

What if this guy runs? Worse yet, what if he doesn't? What if he wants to fight? If he's armed, I won't have a problem shooting him, but what if he's not armed? I'm more afraid of him being unarmed than I am of him being armed. I hate pointing guns at people. This damned society full of lawyers creates more fear in the hunter than the hunted. One of these days, a split-second hesitation to shoot is gonna get me killed. Too many legal ramifications.

What if a cop stops me before I find this guy? I don't need a hassle with the locals. That would be a real laugh if I got booked for a gun law violation. And what about the phony California plate on the car? I wonder if a local cop would understand that one?

It was the same set of doubts every time he went after a bail jumper. Nothing changed. It was the cops on one side, the bad guy on the other and him in the middle. *What a stupid game.*

He leaned over and broke his old single-shot twelve-gauge open. He checked the birdshot shell and felt for the extra one in his pocket. He closed the old gun and smiled. The gun was more of a psychological factor than it was a physical one. True, one shot would make a lot of noise, and maybe even kill someone, but he would never have time to reload and shoot a second time. His pistol would have to do the rest of the job -- if there was more to be done. If he stayed in this business much longer, he would break down and buy one of those pump riot guns.

Baloney. He didn't like a hammerless shotgun. The old-fashioned, break-open, open-hammer, single-shot Savage, with its eighteen and one sixteenth of an inch barrel, was the only shotgun he would ever carry. Besides, this was going to be his last hunt. Things would pick up in his private investigating business soon.

He went over Ernesto's physical description as he mentally matched the two of them in a fight. At five-ten, he and Bill were the same height, but Bill's one hundred seventy-five pounds fell short of Ernesto's weight by almost thirty-five pounds. That, and whoever was with him -- there was always someone with a bail-jumper -- would put Bill at a slight disadvantage in a physical confrontation.

Damn! Maybe he'll be armed and I can just shoot him if he draws down on me. But I don't want to shoot this guy. His biggest crime in life is probably being born poor and stupid.

Bill felt the paper in his shirt pocket, the "Authorization to Arrest" form. *That's about the only comfort I've got, and it isn't much help when the shooting starts.*

He started the engine and drove slowly and deliberately to his destination.

The only time he had ever had to drop the hammer on a fugitive had been in Douglas, Arizona. That had been almost two years ago. Of course, that guy had jumped a hundred-thousand-dollar bond, and was known to be armed and dangerous. Bill should have taken a partner with him on that one, but he hadn't been sure of his information. He was almost as surprised as his fugitive when they met. Fernando Soto Luiz died of an overdose of two, one-hundred-fifty-eight-grain, .357 magnum slugs in the chest.

Bill shuddered as he relived that evening. *Don't think about that kind of stuff right now, you dummy. You can't hesitate if this guy goes froggy.*

He parked his car and re-checked the cartridges in his pistol: Two .38 specials and four .357 magnums, the specials first. He didn't want innocent people hurt by bullets that had a tendency to go through steel. If he didn't get his man with the first panic shot or two, he would have the magnums to fall back on. *Never will get used to that counter-clockwise rotation on a Smith and Wesson cylinder.* He snapped the cylinder back into place, careful to keep the two specials on the right side of the barrel, and holstered the stainless steel Smith. He checked his cuffs, placed his K-bar sheath knife in the small of his back, picked up his shotgun and five-cell flashlight, and stepped into the cool evening air.

He strolled casually down Connoley Street, the shotgun held against his leg so it wouldn't be discernable in the darkness. He was two houses away from Alma Garcia's house.

I wish I could have gotten some information on her. What if there are kids in that house? And what if they're still up? Christ, this is a lousy way to make a buck.

The street was deserted. Maybe none of the neighbors had seen him. He approached the house warily, planning to skirt the front and take up a position near a window on the south side. He would listen there for a few minutes before he made his next move.

Suddenly the yard was awash in light cast by two

large floodlights. *Damn! I forgot about those new motion detectors! Who in the hell would ever have thought a house in this neighborhood would have them?* He heard movement inside the house. *Nothing to do but play it by ear from here on in.* His heart beat wildly as he pulled the shotgun behind his back. He reached under his light jacket and unsnapped the hammer strap on his holster

"Who's there?" The voice was feminine.

Bill stood to the side of the front door and said, "It's Bill Rutledge. A buddy of mine told me Ernie could fix my car. It's just a dinged fender. I'm sorry I dropped by so late, but I just got off work. I couldn't call because you don't have a phone."

"There's no Ernie here. You must have the wrong address."

He looked at the house numbers, only inches from his face. It wasn't the wrong address. He heard whispering on the other side of the door. The curtain in the window moved only slightly, but he caught a glimpse of a male face -- a face that looked just like Ernesto Garcia's. *Maybe I just want it to be Ernesto.*

What the hell do I do now? I'm not sure that's Ernie in there. What if I break down the door and it's not him? He tottered on the brink of indecision only a second.

"Mrs. Garcia, my name is Bill Rutledge. I'm a private investigator from Tucson, Arizona, and I'm here to arrest Ernesto. It's been a long ride, and I'm not going back empty-handed."

He moved the shotgun to the ready. "I've got two men out back, so you might as well come out Ernie. I'll give you five seconds to think it over, then I'm gonna blow a hole in this door I can walk through. Do you understand me?"

There was the sound of whispering voices from behind the door.

"I'm countin', Ernie."

"Don't shoot, man. You're crazy. I'm not Ernesto, man."

Bill stepped back to the corner of the house, into the shadows. "Open the door slowly and step outside. If you're not Ernesto, you've got no problem."

"I'm comin' out, man. Don't shoot. There's kids in here, man."

Bill cocked the hammer on the gun. "Come on out."

The door opened slowly. "Don't shoot, man." Bill's mystery man stepped into the light.

Bill remained in the shadow. "Turn around and face the wall. Put your hands high over your head and lean into it. Move your feet back about a yard and spread your legs."

Bill placed his flashlight on the ground as the man complied with his orders. He then moved quickly up behind the spread-eagled figure and placed the shotgun behind the small of the bigger man's back, careful not to put the barrel too close to his body. Quickly, he frisked him for weapons. The suspect was clean. He stepped back. "Put your hands on your head and lock your fingers together, and slowly -- and I do mean *slowly* --turn around." Bill still wasn't sure. He had studied the picture thoroughly. How could he not be sure? He had to get out of the light. He didn't know what the woman was doing. His knees felt rubbery. He heard the sounds of children speaking Spanish inside the house, almost drowned out by the pounding of his heart in his ears. He knew the pulsing movement at his temples had to be visible, so loud was the noise of the blood pounding against the bone.

"You see?" said the man. "I told you I wasn't Ernesto."

This is crazy! I can't stand out here all night. His heart sounded like a base drum at a football game. He could almost hear the whole band.

"Step into the house real slow. Stay right in front of me and don't move left or right. If you do, you're dead." He followed the bigger man into the house, his hand on the trigger of the shotgun, afraid he might stumble and accidentally shoot a man guilty of nothing more than looking like his suspect, and afraid he might hesitate to shoot if he really had to.

A heavy-set Hispanic woman stood inside the door, a loose-fitting robe draped over her heavy frame, two small and sleepy children by her side. The house smelled of dog. "Please, *señor*, you will frighten my children."

"I'm sorry, ma'am. Would you rather I cuff this guy and haul him off to Tucson without any further discussion?"

"But he is not Ernesto! He has done nothing. What are you doing in my house with a gun in the middle of the night? I should call the police on you."

"Ma'am, I have an arrest authorization in my pocket that says I can bust into any house, at any time, on any day, if I have reason to believe Ernesto is there. I have reason." Bill glanced down the darkened hallway leading to the two bedrooms. "Where's the dog?"

"She is out back," answered the woman.

The youngsters began to cry. "Don't be afraid. I'm not here to hurt anyone." Bill tried to speak soothingly, tried to keep the fear in his chest from manifesting itself in his voice.

The older of the two children, a girl about five, said, "Then why are you pointing a gun at Uncle Pablo?"

"Uncle Pablo?" Bill looked again at the man on the business end of his shotgun. "Let's talk about this, shall we?"

The man kept his hands on his head. "You have the gun. If you say talk, we talk."

"Turn around." Bill reached into the man's rear pocket and pulled out his wallet. "Keep your hands on your head and sit in that chair." He motioned to a worn overstuffed chair in the corner of the room and turned to the woman. "Ma'am, sit down. Keep the kids with you."

Bill waited for them to comply with his request, then opened the wallet one-handed and searched for identification. The only things in the wallet were one California lottery ticket and a driver's license. He looked up at his prisoner. "Pablo Garcia?"

"Ernesto is my brother."

"Where is he?"

"He's not here."

Bill moved a step in Pablo's direction, pointing the gun at his chest. "I asked you where he *is*, not where he isn't."

The older child shrieked in fear.

"We don't know," said Alma.

Bill faced her. "You expect me to believe that? You've bailed him out of jail before. He always comes running to you when he gets into trouble with the law."

She sighed. "He was here four days ago. I told him to go away. We have been divorced for two years now. He is not good for the children." She looked near tears.

"Where did he go?"

"I don't really know. He said he was going to San Francisco, but he may have been lying." Her lips quivered.

"Does he have friends or relatives up there?"

She shook her head. "No friends that I know of, and no relatives."

"Where did he get his money? You give him a few bucks?"

She exchanged a quick glance with Pablo, who still sat unmoving, his hands on his head, fingers interlocked. Alma Garcia broke into tears. "He took everything we had. Pablo was here and tried to reason with him, but he has a gun and he threatened to kill all of us if we didn't give him money. We have nothing to eat in the house; the children are very hungry." She shook her head. "He is a desperate man, *Senor.*"

Bill glanced again at the empty wallet. He looked at Pablo. "Take your hands down. Relax. Don't make me sorry I believe you, or I'll shoot you -- fair enough?" He uncocked the gun and tossed the wallet to Pablo.

"What Alma says is the truth, man." Pablo dropped his hands to his lap. "Ernesto took what little money we both had. He has a .22 magnum pistol -- one of those cheap models. The children have had very little to eat. I don't get paid until next Friday."

Bill stood and walked to the refrigerator. He opened it slowly. A half-empty-Tupperware container held a small portion of pinto beans. There was nothing else. He looked at Pablo. "There's no milk in here for the kids."

"We have no money until I get paid," said Pablo.

"What about welfare or something?"

Alma stuck out her chin. "We don't need welfare. We'll have money on payday."

Bill narrowed his eyes. "And what are you going to feed those kids until then? Pride?"

"We'll make it. It is none of your business."

Bill looked at the faces of the two wide-eyed children, held tightly to their mother's sides by her heavy arms. He slammed the refrigerator door shut. "You're right. It's none of my business." He pulled the "Authorization to Arrest" form from his pocket. "See this? This *is* my business." He handed her one of his business cards. "If you hear from Ernesto, call me. Collect." He wanted to offer more of his opinion about Ernesto, up to and including the sex drive of his mother, but he held his urge in check. The kids would be the only victims of a verbal assault on their father. He pulled his wallet from his pocket and counted out two twenties and a ten. "This is a locator fee. If you call me, you earned it. If you don't, then it was just a bad investment on my part. Now buy those kids some food." He moved to the door and stopped to face them.

"*Adios.*"

Alma held the money tightly in her hand; tears streamed down her heavy face, falling into space from her double chin. "*Muchas gracias, oh, muchas gracias. Vaya con Dios.* May God bless you. You are a kind man."

"Yeah. And stupid too," said Bill as he opened the door and stepped into the night.

Bill sat in the restaurant at the Orange Avenue exit and counted his money as he sipped his coffee and smoked a cigarette. He hadn't even searched the house. *What if ol' Ernie had been there all the time? Naw. He wasn't there. A lot of times in this business you've gotta go by your gut feeling. My gut says he's not there. Damn! I feel sorry for those kids.* He looked down at the money in his hand. If he didn't eat until he got home, he'd have just enough of his expense money left to get to Tucson. Of course, he'd have to pay back the indemnitor the fifty dollars he had given to Alma, but what the hell? There was always someone jumping bail. He'd make it up on the next one.

He took a drag on his cigarette and stared at a brown stain on the wall. *It's good to see you again, old friend.*

CHAPTER 2

Bill awoke to the ringing of the telephone in his study. He awoke to that particular phone, because that's where he had fallen asleep the night before. He glanced up from his prone position to see an empty bourbon bottle on the floor next to his head.

He remembered sitting down to make that big decision to quit his private investigating business -- more specifically the bounty hunting end of it -- and sip a shot or two of warm whiskey while he thought it over. As he pondered what he would do to earn a living, he dipped deeper into the bottle. The decision wasn't really all that easy. He refused to work domestic investigations; all of the insurance companies were tied up by other P.I. agencies; he wouldn't work for an attorney if it were the only way to survive, and the criminal end of his business had always been slow. From his point of view, most people accused of a crime were stone-cold guilty and felt little need to spend money on a P.I. to prove that which could not be proven.

Just as he realized he was talking himself out of the private investigating business altogether, he finished the last of the bottle and laid down on the carpeted floor to mull over his job skills. That's when the lights went out.

The phone continued to ring. He crawled to the small table supporting it, wondering why he bothered.

The inside of his mouth felt like dried cotton. He was sure if he spoke; no one would be able to understand what he said. *The damn thing will probably quit ringing about the time I get to it anyway.*

In the three days since he had returned from San Diego, all he had done was clean up old paperwork -- not much for producing revenue. He reached up and grabbed the phone, knocking the receiver to the floor. Rather than touch it again with his hands, he crawled to it and lay his head on it, ear to the receiver. "Bill's Bounty Service."

"This is the operator. I have a collect call for Bill Rutledge from Alma Garcia. Will you accept the charges?"

Who is Alma Garcia? He rolled his eyes at the beamed ceiling. "Sure, operator."

"One moment while I connect you."

"Hello, is this Mr. Rutledge?"

"Yeah, that's me. What can I do for you?"

"Do you remember? You come look for Ernesto in San Diego."

Bill sat up on the carpet, grabbing the handset and holding it to his ear. His mind was as clear as a Saskatchewan summer day. "Yes, Alma. I remember. How thoughtful of you to call." *Collect, of course.* "Have you heard from Ernesto?"

"Yes. He call to say he sorry and he coming back to Tucson to see his attorney."

"What for?"

"I think he want turn himself in."

"When?" Bill's heart began to race. Just the thought of the chase was enough to build his adrenaline.

"He be there today. Soon, I think. I told him about

you and how you gave us money to eat. I thin' he is going to call you and let you bring him in."

"You're kidding?"

"No. He told me."

"Anything else?"

"No. I just want to thank you one more time."

"You're welcome. You earned it today."

"Okay. Goodbye."

"Bye." He slowly put the receiver back on the hook. The plungers were barely depressed when the phone rang again. "Bill's Bounty Service."

"I like to speak to Bill Rutledge please."

"This is Bill Rutledge."

"I'm Ernesto Garcia. I'm going to turn myself in. If you give half your bounty to my wife and kids, I turn myself in to you. If not, I walk into the jail and you get nothing."

"I don't do blackmail or make deals with a bounty."

"You lose then, mister." The phone went dead.

Bill rushed to his briefcase leaning against the wall and opened it quickly. He jerked out a legal file folder marked "Ernesto Garcia" and spread the contents on the floor, rummaging through them quickly. His hand lingered on one of the documents. A smile spread across his face as he read it. He looked at the inanimate telephone sitting silently atop the table. "No, Ernie, old man, you lose." He grabbed a set of car keys from the pegboard just inside his four-car garage, jumped into his '57 T-Bird and created a cloud of dust as he sped down his long dirt driveway.

Bill sat in a little nook next to the entrance of the

lobby, his back to the wall, the door on his right. A secretary sat hidden behind the tall, arched counter with the words "Public Defender" neatly chiseled into a glued-on sign at the end near the door. He picked up a magazine and began to leaf through it. Ernesto probably hadn't had time to get here yet but it didn't really matter. If he walked through the entrance, his back would be towards Bill. If he came from one of the attorney's offices, he would have to walk within two feet of Bill's chair.

He dropped the magazine and rummaged through the stack of professional journals. *Why don't they ever have Hot Rod Magazine or Field and Stream in waiting rooms anymore?* The door on his right opened and a man and woman entered. The woman was Ernesto's sister. He had spoken to her early on in his search.

Bill recognized Ernesto from the mug shot the instant he passed through the door. He remained sitting until his bounty walked by him then, still seated, said. "Psst. Hey Ernie. You're under arrest."

Ernesto spun around and saw him sitting there, handcuffs dangling from his belt on his right side and a three-inch-barreled .357 magnum Smith and Wesson on his left.

Bill motioned to the chair at his side. "Have a seat." He smiled.

"Oh shit. Oh shit, man. I just wanna see my lawyer, man."

"You holdin', Ernie?" asked Bill. Ernesto's sister showed no alarm. She was probably the one who had talked him into turning himself in. Bill wasn't concerned about her. If anything, she was on his side.

"Shit no, man. I got no weapons. Are you crazy?"

"Sit." Bill patted the seat of the chair next to him.

Reluctantly, and with hunched shoulders, Ernesto sat in the chair. "You gonna let me see my lawyer, man?"

"I ought to cuff you and drag you in right now."

"Why, man? What did I do?"

"I didn't like your attitude on the phone."

"Shit, man, I'm sorry. I was just trying to help out my ol' lady the only way I can right now, man. You'd do the same thing."

"Maybe, but I'd a' been a bit more polite about it. You put her in the position she was in in the first place. Or did that little detail slip your mind?"

"Let me see my lawyer, man. Gimme a break."

Bill smiled. "Okay, Ernie. But I'm with you every minute."

By the time they left the Public Defender's office, Bill's opinion of lawyers had fallen to a new low. During the course of Ernesto's conversation with the attorney, Bill had learned that Ernesto had simply walked out of the courthouse during a recess in his trial. His attorney had told Ernesto that there was no way any verdict but guilty would result. He had then said that he was going to get them some coffee and would be gone about five minutes. If Ernesto wasn't there when he got back, he would understand. *I hope that damned lawyer gets caught at something -- anything -- and he jumps bail. I'll do that one for free.*

Bill sat in the booking room at the Pima County Jail, finishing the booking form. He signed his name and turned to Ernesto at his side. "Okay, Ernie, you'll be in the good hands of these fine deputies from here on out. I wish you the best, and whenever it's all over, try walking a little closer to the right side of the law. Oh, by the way, I'll send your ex-wife half of the bounty."

Ernesto looked up at him. "But why? Why did you go through all of this trouble if you were going to give her half of the money?"

"I wasn't. I told you, I don't make deals with blackmailers, and I never mess with a bounty. Once I've got the money, I can do whatever I damn well please with it."

"Are you serious?"

"Serious as a heart attack, Ernie, ol' man. Don't worry about it. Half of the bounty will be on its way to San Diego this afternoon." He stood.

Ernesto reached up and tugged on a belt loop. "Hey, man, sit down a second."

Bill sat. "What, Ernie?"

Ernie leaned close. "Listen, man, you're not such an asshole."

"Coming from you, Ernie, that means a lot to me."

"Hey, man, cut the shit. I'm about to turn you on to something good."

"What's that, Ernie?"

"The biggest bounty you ever heard of."

Christ! Another war story. "Go ahead, Ernie. I'm listening."

"There's this guy and this girl, see? They jumped bail big time in L.A. last week. Well, they didn't actually jump bail yet -- their arraignment isn't until day after tomorrow -- but that don't matter. They're gone, man. Like they're south of here, you know what I mean?"

"What's the rap?"

"Oowie. It's as long as your arm: possession, possession for sale, ADW, ag. assault, two counts of attempted murder, felony escape, and murder."

"Ernie, you been smokin' some real bad weed, son. Charges like that would put bond outa sight."

"One million each."

Bill was getting interested. "One million each? Where the hell did they get collateral to post that kind of bond?"

"They signed power of attorney on some prime ocean property in Malibu. It was free and clear, you know what I mean?"

"The bondsman will probably forget about them and go after the property."

Ernie smiled. "No shit. Only trouble is, they were originally arrested under the wrong names. They don't own the property."

"Some bondsman just went broke. It happens every day."

Ernesto shook his head. "No, man, this guy ain't goin' broke. It's AAAA Bail Bonds. He's big time in L.A., man. He's makin' a fortune out there. He'll be lookin' for 'em, you can bet on it."

"I've been in Mexico twice lookin' for bounties and the last time was the last time. Thanks for the hot tip, Ernie. Maybe next time."

"But I know where they're gonna be, man."

Bill leaned into him. "Ernie, how come you know so damn much about these people?"

"I put them up one night on the money I took from Alma -- just to tide them over until they were able to get ahold of some of their cash -- and the bastards split on me early the next morning."

Bill stood. "What a surprise. Thanks anyway, Ernie. Don't worry about the money. I told you I was gonna send Alma half, and I will." He turned to leave.

"Hey, man, I'm serious. Check it out. Their real names are Julie Short and Mike Sturdivan. The bondsman doesn't even know that yet, man. I'm giving you exclusive information here. They were booked under Elizabeth Wells and Michael Stanley. And they gonna be layin' low in a little town called Guaymas."

"Thanks, Ernie. I'll check it out. You take care of yourself, you hear?"

"I'm tellin' ya straight, man. I'm tellin' ya straight."

Bill hurried out the door as quickly as the electronic lock was deactivated. He had a bounty to collect at Great American Bail Bonds.

Louisa Contreras counted out the money in twenties. Louisa was a large woman with a young face, and most of the time it was smiling. Bill wasn't sure if it was because she was happy or because she forgot she was sad. He'd never known a person -- male or female -- that was as rattle-brained and as unorganized as Louisa. Chasing bail-jumpers for her had cost him a lot of money in the past eighteen months, mostly as a result of incorrect information on his bounty.

Despite her many imperfections, she was honest to a fault, and as good-hearted as anyone alive. Bill was quite fond of her, though he never presented anything less than his toughest front while in her presence.

"Five forty. Five fifty." She pushed the small stack of bills at him, a smile stretching from ear to ear.

"Thanks, Louisa. You got anything else?"

"Oh! Don' say that. What you think? All I wanna do is chase bail-jumpers?"

"I'm the one who chases 'em."

"But I have to pay you."

"Yeah, and not enough either."

"It's same as everybody else."

"They don't pay enough either." He paused a moment. "Say, Louisa, you ever hear of AAAA Bail Bonds in L.A.?"

She laughed. "You watch college football?"

He nodded.

"You ever hear of the Arizona Wildcats?"

"Couldn't you have just said yes?"

"Now you understand me better."

"*Si*. So I do. Well, if something comes up, you've got my number -- if the Phone Company hasn't disconnected it yet."

"Why you don' sell one of your cars?"

Bill gave her an injured look.

"They are old and junky, but maybe you could find some kid with lots of money and no brains to buy one of them."

"Louisa! You've cut me to the quick. I need those cars, besides, they're all classics." He added a look of hurt to his expression but quickly covered it with a smile.

"Most of them look more like relics. Why you need five cars anyway?"

"Six."

"Six."

"Because someday, when I get outa this business and get rich and famous, I'll have a good start on a car collection."

"They are all hot rods."

"What good is a slow car?"

"Yours go too fast, especially when you drive them. How old are you now anyway?"

"Forty-five, give or take a year or two. Why?"

"It's time you sell all those hot rods and buy one good car."

"Louisa, my dear, you have handed me the ultimate insult. Next time you need someone with a fast car to chase down a speedy bail-jumper, remember this conversation. With that, I bid you *adios*."

She giggled as he walked out the door, her chest and upper arms bouncing about like Jell-O on a roller coaster.

He jumped into his 1957 T-Bird and drove west, toward the Tucson Mountains. He'd been lucky to find such a nice piece of property back when he'd had the money and the credit to buy it. Ten acres with a house and guest house, both hand-built in the forties by the original owner. The four-car garage he'd added himself before things went sour in his machine shop business.

He should have gotten out of that business when his biggest customer -- a high-tech electronic firm -- pulled up stakes and consolidated its facilities back east, but he hung on for two years and lost everything. Everything but his house. He struggled to make the payments, but it was worth it to him. Someday, if he ever met a woman he thought was worth marrying, the house would be a great place to raise a football team -- or a cheerleading squad -- except people don't think in those terms these days.

He parked the T-Bird outside, next to a creosote

bush, and stepped into the house. He went directly to the phone and dialed L.A. information, then the number to AAAA Bail Bonds.

"AAAA Bail Bonds. How may we be of service?" said a female voice.

"My name is Bill Rutledge and I'm calling from Tucson, Arizona. I'd like to talk to the owner please."

"One moment, sir. I'll transfer your call."

Bill thought of the small, two or three person bonds offices in Tucson and smiled. *Yeah, Ernesto, you're right. Business must be pretty good in L.A.*

"This is Bernie Heinkel, may I help you?"

"I don't know just yet. I'm trying to find out if I've got the right place. Did you bond out an Elizabeth Wells and a Michael Stanley recently?"

"Who are you, sir?"

"Oh, I'm sorry. My name is Bill Rutledge. I'm a private investigator. I understand you bailed these folks out and they appear tomorrow or the next day. Is that right?"

"What is your interest, Mr. Rutledge?"

"I'm a bounty hunter, and I have reason to believe you're going to be in need of one here shortly."

"I appreciate your concern, Mr. Rutledge, but I have ample collateral to cover the bond. Will there be anything else?" His voice was smug.

"I think you better jot down my number in case you change your mind. Your collateral may not be worth too much when push comes to shove. Whoever the real Mr. Stanley is, I'm pretty sure he isn't going to like it when you try to foreclose with a power of attorney signed by the guy who happened to have his stolen wallet when the police picked him up."

"Where did you get your information?" A shadow of doubt crept into the voice.

"Can't say. I'm not positive that I'm even right but, if I am, I may know where to find these two. I've got good references here in Tucson if you want to check me out. If you find what I'm saying is true, I'd appreciate a call. My number is -- you got a pencil?"

"Go ahead." Now the voice was tainted with a hint of irritation.

"520-555-8809. You got it?"

"I have it, Mr Rutledge, but in all candor, I doubt I'll be calling you, even if what you say is true. I have several people here in Los Angeles that I use on a regular basis."

"It's your business, Mr. Heinkel. But remember, I'm the one who knows where they are. Give it a thought. If I'm not in the office, just leave a message. Thanks for your time, sir."

Two days later, he got the call. "Private Investigations."

"Mr. Rutledge?"

He recognized the voice. "You may call me Bill, sir."

"This is Bernie Heinkel. I don't know where you got your information, but it was accurate."

"Even the part about the wallet?"

"All of it."

"I made that part up. Couldn't figure how else he could have pulled it off."

"Very good, Mr. Rutledge--"

"Bill."

"--Bill, but I would like to meet with you and discuss the terms of an arrangement."

"Your welcome to meet with me, sir, but the terms of the arrangement are the standard. No changes."

"But that's ridiculous! Surely you don't expect a full seven percent on a bond of this size."

Bill smiled into the receiver. "I like you already, Bernie."

"What happened to 'Mr. Heinkel'?"

"He left with the seven percent. I thought I told you I had at least two days experience. In case I didn't, I'll let you know now, this will be my second case -- not my first. I work for ten percent and I pay my own way. If I don't bring 'em in, you don't pay me a dime."

"Impossible on this one. I've got men willing to do it for ten thousand each bounty."

"You know, Bernie, that's probably a good idea. Let those guys have a shot at it for a while. When they finally admit they can't bring 'em in -- call me but, for your sake, do it before the bond forfeits. If you lose my number, you can find it in the yellow pages under 'Investigators'. They didn't have a category for bounty hunters.

"Oh, by the way, I'm leaving day after tomorrow for a two-week vacation to the Virgin Islands, so you'll have to reach me before I go, or wait until I get back. If you wait until the day I'm ready to leave, there'll be a one thousand-dollar inconvenience charge for me having to cancel my vacation plans at the last minute. I'll reimburse you when I bring in the bounties -- just to show my good faith."

"I don't think I can work with you. Your attitude is bad. And you have no respect."

"Oh, I've got respect all right. I've never met you and I know you. We'll get along fine, once you quit playin' games. You got the money, but I got the cards. I don't know what kind of people you got working for you over there, but if any one of 'em had the grit, he'd set you straight, and maybe you wouldn't act like such a jerk. Have a nice day, Bernie." He hung up the phone and sat in the overstuffed chair at its side.

He trembled from rage and fear. Rage at the superior attitude displayed by Bernie and fear that he had gone too far and the man would never call him back -- even if it meant losing the bond. *No. No way. His pride isn't worth that much to him. He's not as stupid as I am. And I've been to Mexico. He won't get them out of there unless he finds a lucky, crazy man.*

CHAPTER 3

Bill heard the soft rumble of a throaty V-8 draw nearer as a car rolled slowly up the dirt driveway to his house. He straightened up from under the hood of his 1970 Hemi Challenger and placed his wrench in a fork of the mesquite providing him shade. The bright blue of Tom Lassiter's '57 Chevy nearly blinded him as the sun's rays bounced off the metallic particles in the paint. He smiled and wiped his hands on an old T-shirt.

Tom was one of the few people he knew who enjoyed the older cars. In addition to the one he was driving, he owned another '57 -- a Nomad station wagon -- with the loudest yellow paint job Bill had ever seen.

As the Chevy rounded the last bend in the drive, Bill noticed the top was down and neatly tucked under a custom tonneau cover. And he noticed Tom wasn't alone. Tom stopped the car behind the Challenger, gunned the engine once and turned off the ignition switch.

"Every time I see you, you're working on this Challenger. What's the matter with it this time?" Greeted Tom as he stepped from his car.

Bill jerked a thumb at the engine. "It's the hemi. Lots of horsepower, but you gotta work on 'em every time you start 'em up to keep 'em right." He glanced at the blonde in the middle of the blue and white tuck-and-roll seat, then made a more careful study of the redhead in the back. "What brings you up here today? Slummin'?"

"Bill, I want you to meet a couple of friends of mine." He looked at the blonde and said, "This is Connie." He jerked his head to the rear. "And that Irish fireball in the back seat is Laura O'leary."

Bill nodded. "Nice to meet you ladies. Get out and stretch your legs. Tom, you know where the fridge is. I didn't expect company. There may be a couple a beers and some iced tea."

Tom opened the door and Connie scooted out the driver's door. Laura opened her own door and stepped out. "I was telling the girls here about a friend of mine who does bounty hunting for a living. They didn't believe me, so I thought I'd show 'em what a real tough *hombre* looks like."

Bill felt the heat in his cheeks rise above the heat of the late spring morning. "I told you, that's only a sideline. I'm a private investigator."

"Yeah, I know. And a bounty hunter." He faced the women. "Well, there he is, girls. I told you he wasn't anything special to look at."

Bill looked at Connie. She was tall and supple and sexy, and stupid looking. That's the way Tom liked his girlfriends. A marriage gone sour after ten years drove Tom to the camp of the "permanent" bachelor club. He avoided women with brains like most men would avoid the plague. His ex-wife was an assistant professor at the University of Arizona.

Laura was a different story. She didn't seem to fit in. She was attractive, but it was more of a cute kind of attractive as opposed to the sex that seemed to ooze from Connie's every pore. She was four or five inches shorter than Connie's five-feet-eight, and with her upturned nose and fiery red hair, she seemed a contradiction of description. Both women wore cut-off jeans and colorful cotton blouses.

"Oh, he's not so bad," said Connie.

"Thanks," said Bill dryly.

"You really make a living as a bounty hunter?" she asked.

Bill shook his head. "About forty percent of it."

Connie's eyes wandered about the property. "Looks to me like you're doing all right."

Bill smiled. "I don't know what ol' Tom here has told you, but I bought this place years ago when I was in the chips. Been fighting to hold onto it for the last few years."

"You want a beer?" asked Tom.

Bill shook his head. "No, you go ahead. Let me finish buttoning this thing up and I'll be with you in a few minutes." He turned to the women. "Make yourselves at home. I'll be done in a little bit."

Tom walked into the house, Connie hanging all over him. Bill turned and leaned over the engine. He snapped the distributor cap in place and bumped the remote starter switch while moving the accelerator rod once. The engine roared to life. He bumped the accelerator a couple of quick times and smiled at the instant response of the big 426 cubic inch engine.

"Sounds good to me."

Bill jumped at the sound of the voice and bumped his head on the underside of the hood. He turned to see Laura smiling as he rubbed the back of his head gently. "I thought you went inside with Tom and Connie. You took me by surprise."

She laughed, showing two perfect rows of white teeth. "So I see. Are you okay?"

Bill smiled, more to hide the pain than to be friendly. "I've been better. But I've been a lot worse. No complaint here." He pulled his hand from his hair and found his fingers red with blood.

"Oh, my god. You hit that thing harder than I thought you did."

Bill put his fingers back in his hair and massaged the cut. "It's all right."

"I'm sorry. I didn't mean to laugh, but you looked so funny when you jumped..."

"I'm fine. And I'm sure it looked funny."

"You better clean it up."

"It's not worth bothering with. Really." He turned and leaned over the engine. Laura said nothing more, but went into the house to join the others.

He had just finished adjusting the carburetor, turned off the ignition, and turned to put his screwdriver into the toolbox at his feet when he saw Laura standing next to it with a bowl of steaming water and a clean wash cloth. *Christ. A Florence Nightingale. Where does Tom find these broads?*

"I caused it. The least I can do is fix it. Sit down under the tree and let me clean that cut."

"I'm telling you, it's nothing. Forget it."

"Look, Mister Bounty Hunter, I know you're bad and nothing bothers you, but it bothers me, so why don't you placate me and have a seat?"

Placate? Placate? I wonder if Tom knows this one can speak English? I better tell him first chance I get. He shook his head and sat with his back to the tree.

Laura squatted next to him and dipped the cloth in the water. As she daubed at the hair hiding the cut, her breast rubbed against his shoulder lightly. He wondered if she were a little shy and this was her way of making a play.

"You smell good. What's that you're wearing?"

She moved her body back a few inches. "Soap," she said coldly.

Bill sat silently, feeling much the fool for another two or three minutes, while she finished cleaning the wound. Laura made no further attempt at conversation. She dropped the bloody cloth in the bowl and stood silently, her tanned legs only inches from his face.

He looked up to find her staring down at him. "What?"

She said nothing.

Bill stood. He looked at a branch on the mesquite. "Well, you *do* smell good." He thought he caught the glimpse of a smile as she turned and walked back to the house. *Soap. Why didn't I think of that?*

Tom stuck his head out of the door as Laura stepped by him. "Hey, Bill. You got a long distance phone call. Some guy from L.A. Talks funny. Jewish accent."

Bill's heart thumped as he ran for the house. He stepped inside and picked up the receiver. "This is Bill, may I help you?"

"This is Bernie Heinkel."

Bill smiled and put his index finger to his lips, signaling the others to be quiet. "Yes, Bernie. What can I do for you?"

"I don't want to play games, Mr. Rutledge --"

"Bill."

"Very well, Bill then. I'm calling about the subject you broached the other day. I may want to consult with you on this case."

"Consult? No. I don't think so, Bernie. You know, I'm beginning to like you more every time we talk. You've got a unique approach to things."

There was a short pause. Bill thought he heard a voice in the background. Bernie said, "Be reasonable. I can't afford ten percent on this one. The collateral I have is zero. Do you understand me? This comes out of my pocket. It will break me."

"I'm real sorry to hear that, Bern. I really am. But I work these two for one hundred thousand apiece or I don't work 'em."

He heard the voice in the background again. "What're you trying to do, kill me? What makes it so tough to run these two down?"

"Nice try, Bern, but you get nothing. You can tell that guy with you, if he's going after these two on a company clock, he'd better be sure his will is current and his life insurance is paid up."

"Okay, okay. How much do you want to tell me where they are?"

Bill thought it over. *Why be greedy? Half a sure thing is better than maybe all of nothing.* "One hundred thousand."

"You're the one who should be in jail, Mr. Rutledge."

"Bill."

"I don't care what you call yourself. This is

36

blackmail."

"Now, Bern, old buddy, relax. Take a deep breath and loosen up. I'm not forcing you to accept anything. As a matter-of-fact, I'm beginning to regret I ever called you. Please accept my apology. You're probably right. You big city boys can handle this much more economically than a cowboy like me. It was nice talking with you, Bern." Bill gently hung up the phone.

"What was that all about?" asked Tom.

"Just a case I offered to work on."

"Must be some case," said Connie. "You were sure tossing around some big numbers."

Laura looked at him curiously.

Tom said, "C'mon, Bill, lay it out, man. This is a big time bail-jumper, isn't it?"

"No sense talking about it. The man is cheap. He won't pay a fair price."

"What did they do?" asked Connie.

"They're accused of dealing drugs and killin' folks."

"Did they do it?"

Bill looked at Connie. *I think Tom went overboard on this one. She's really dumb.* "I don't know. Probably. Most people indicted are guilty."

"So why do you want so much money to bring in two people?" asked Tom. "Hell, I saw you bring in those two Mexican dudes for a grand total of eleven hundred dollars, and I gotta tell ya, I don't think they come much meaner than those two."

Bill shrugged. "They were easy. I just waited for 'em to get drunk and pass out."

"So why not do the same with these two?"

"Is there any beer left? I believe I would like a cold

one," said Bill. He started for the refrigerator.

"I'll get it. Tell us about the two Mexicans," said Connie.

"Thanks. There's no more to tell."

Tom persisted. "What about these two? Why so much money?"

"They're out on a million dollars bail apiece."

Tom whistled.

"And they're in Mexico," added Bill.

"Oh." Tom took a sip of his beer. "I remember the last time you went into Mexico. It didn't turn out so good."

"What happened?" Connie was back in the living room with Bill's beer.

"He damn near got killed."

"It was a lousy neighborhood, in a druggie town," said Bill.

"Where was that?" asked Connie.

"Naco," answered Tom. He looked at Bill. "These two aren't in Naco are they?"

"Guaymas."

"Guaymas! Hell, we could all drive down there for the weekend and have a good time as tourists. We could pick them up on the way out of town. They'd more than pay for the trip."

Bill shook his head. "You been watchin' too many movies, Tom."

"Hell, Guaymas is a pretty clean town as far as Mexican towns go."

"Yeah, but I still got the gun laws I gotta break, and once I get 'em, I gotta get 'em back across the border and over to L.A."

"Yeah, but if we went with you, it would be a

perfect cover. They would never expect a bunch of tourists to be out chasing down a bounty. We wouldn't have to be in on the actual bust, but we could at least make it easier for you to get around without making it look suspicious."

"That sounds like fun to me. I've never been to Guaymas," said Connie.

Bill stared out the window. *It would be a great cover. And they wouldn't have to be in any danger. I can leave them when I'm ready to make the bust, and they can drive back in a separate car. It wouldn't be like Naco.* He looked at them. Tom sat, his eyebrows arched in a question mark. Connie pleaded with a sad-cow look. Laura stood near the picture window, expressionless.

He could count on Tom's cool head if he really needed him. And, of course, he would offer to pay them something. "It might work."

A smile spread over Tom's face. "Of course it'll work."

"If I get 'em back to L.A. and collect the bounty, I'll give you ten thousand apiece. You don't have to do anything but pretend to be tourists with me. When I locate 'em, you drive back in your own car and the rest is up to me."

Connie squealed, "Count me in!" She cuddled up to Tom on the love seat.

"You know I'm ready," said Tom.

"What about you, Laura?" asked Tom. He jerked his head at Bill. "He won't bite. He treats his women real good. A little old-fashioned sometimes, but he treats 'em real good."

"Tom, you never will grow up. You're talking about

it like it's a weekend vacation," said Laura.

"It is. For us. Bill here's gonna do all the work. All we're gonna do is go fishing and dancing and eat some of the best shrimp in the world." He paused and his expression became serious. "And I know Bill. He's going if this Bern guy calls him back. All we're doing is making it a little safer for him."

"I'll go, but I've got to call the pa...work and let them know I'll be out a few days," said Laura.

Bill smiled. "Thanks, but I wouldn't make that call until I hear from the bondsman, and that may not happen. I think I just made him mad." He looked at Tom. "You're not taking your fifty-seven down there, are you?"

"Not on your life. If we decide to go, I'll switch cars when we go home to pack."

The phone rang. Bill picked it up. "Private Investigations." He smiled to the others in the room when he heard Bernie's voice.

"This is Bernie Heinkel. I'll let you have the case, but I'm telling you right now, I'm puttin' every bail recovery agent in the business on it too. Whoever gets them first gets the bounty."

Sonofabitch. "Have it your way, Bern. If you want me to get involved now, I'll need that thousand dollars I mentioned for the late notice, a certified copy of the bond, a copy of the bench warrant if there is one, clear pictures of the subjects, all pertinent info on said subjects, an authorization to arrest on your behalf, a notarized statement to the effect I'm to receive ten percent of the bond on each subject returned, and your blessing -- but I don't need that last part in writing."

"I'm not in the habit of laying out advances."

"You were advised of the need for a quick decision. Now, do you want the address to Federal Express it to or not?"

"Give it to me." Bernie's voice was strained. "You better bring them back, Mr. Rutledge."

"Bern, I want the thousand dollars net. Don't take out the Federal Express charges."

Bill watched Nogales, Sonora disappear from his rear-view mirror. Tom's late model Thunderbird followed only a few hundred yards behind his 1969 GTO convertible. They were in Mexico. As soon as Federal Express had delivered the package from Bernie they had jumped into the cars and headed south. Laura sat quietly in the passenger seat next to him, taking in the countryside. She had spoken only once or twice since they had left Tucson. He was beginning to feel a little uncomfortable.

"I really do appreciate you coming along. I think you'll like the food in Guaymas. Tom wasn't kidding. They do have some mighty fine shrimp there."

"Don't you think you're overdoing it with that Hawaiian shirt?" she asked.

"Is that what's bothering you? I just put it on for the trip down. When we go out tonight, I'll wear something different. You feel better now?"

She smiled. "It's not really that bad. I guess I seem to be the only one who remembers why you're coming down here."

Bill shook his head. "Oh no, I remember real well. We're gonna eat drink and be merry, right?"

She laughed. "Don't you take anything seriously?"

"Sure."
"What?"
"Breakfast."
Again she laughed. "See what I mean?"
"I'm serious."
"How are you going to get these people to come back with you?"
"If they don't want to come along peaceably, I'll point a gun at 'em and put 'em in handcuffs."
"I didn't see any guns or handcuffs."
Bill grinned. "Good. Trust me. They're here."
She stared out the window at the passing scrub oak and cedar.
"It's a pretty day, isn't it?" he said.
"It sure is. When do you think we'll be in Guaymas?"
"A little before dark I'd guess."
"When will you start looking for them?"
"Oh, I'll be looking for them the minute we get there, but I won't go out of my way until we've seen a little bit of the town. That's why you guys came down here, isn't it?"
She turned her attention from the countryside and looked at him. "To tell you the truth, I don't know why I came along."
Bill smiled. "You sure do a lot for a guy's ego, you know that? How old are you anyway?"
She returned his smile. "That's not the kind of thing a gentleman asks a lady."
"I'll give you the lady part, but I think you're overdoing it in my case."
"I'm thirty-five."

"What kind of work you do?"

She seemed to hesitate. "I'm in communications. How old are you?"

"Communications? What kind?"

"You're dodging the question."

"Forty-six."

"And you do this for a living?"

He sighed. "Yeah, it is kind of stupid, isn't it?"

"Surely you can do something else? I mean, you don't have to do this, do you?"

"No. But I'm kind of like everybody else, I guess -- you get into something and you get comfortable with what you're doing -- you just get into a rut, I guess."

"How long have you known Tom?"

He thought about the question. "About ten years, I think. We don't get to spend a lot of time together, but I think he's a great guy. Can't say much for his taste in women most of the time, but that's none of my business. How long you known him?"

"Sometimes it seems like too long."

"You don't seem like his type -- no offense intended -- I meant it as a compliment."

She laughed. "He said you were to the point. I'm not his type. I'm...more like a friend."

He glanced at her, then returned his attention to the road. "That's nice to know."

"You ever been married, Bill?"

He waited a long time before answering. "Yeah. Yeah, I was married once -- for almost ten years."

"What happened?"

"I spent more time at work than I should have. Tried to build up financial security and all that stuff. I worked so long and so hard, I forgot what I was working for. I didn't take time to smell the roses. She filed for divorce on the grounds of desertion. She was right."

"What happened to her?"

"I don't know. I heard she went back to California where she was from. Probably met up with an old boyfriend and lived happily ever after. I hope so. She deserved it. She was a fine woman. Beautiful too. She came from money. She'll be all right."

"Any kids?"

"Nope. I was always too busy building a future for one to get down to the real business of makin' one." He glanced over at her again. "How 'bout you? You been married?"

She nodded. "Three years. We were just divorced last year. Tom thought it would be good for me to start getting out. I haven't dated since the divorce."

"Kids?"

She shook her head. "No. And I'm glad. That would have been just something else to fight about. He drank a lot."

"I like a shot of bourbon now and again myself."

"He got mean when he drank. He used to beat me and run around with other women. I put up with it for a while, but then I grew up. It was tough."

"Sorry."

"Don't be. I'm not. I'm a better person for it all."

Bill couldn't imagine Laura standing still while some drunk beat her. He cleared his throat. "There's a little spot in the road up here. You wanna stop and get a coke or something?"

"Sounds like a good idea to me."

CHAPTER 4

The sun was low on the horizon when they pulled into Guaymas. The pink rays of light bouncing from the gentle swells offshore colored the buildings an incandescent shade of orange. Tall masts swayed back and forth with the water as bows creaked softly from the constantly changing pressures. The GTO's convertible top was down as Bill led Tom by little more than a block into the peaceful seaport town

"It's beautiful," said Laura.

"Even the Mexicans can have a pretty town now and then," said Bill, a smile spread across his face.

"It could sure put a person in a laid-back, easy-going mood. No wonder the Mexicans are never in a hurry. It almost feels like someone has cast a spell over me."

Bill made a sudden left turn, then glanced sheepishly at Laura. "Sorry. I almost missed our turn. We gotta get checked in by six, just to be safe."

She smiled. "You sure know how to bring a mood back to business, don't you?"

Bill wasn't certain what she meant. During the long drive from Tucson, he found himself thinking of her in several different ways. She was attractive, intelligent, witty, graceful, and kind. That much he had learned and he wondered again how Tom had ever managed to get close enough to her to maintain any kind of relationship.

"Not on purpose. I promise."

Two blocks down the street, only a block from the waterfront, he pulled under the archway of *La Hacienda*, one of the finer hotels in Guaymas. Tom parked behind him, and the four of them walked into the lobby.

The plush red carpet and the hand-polished mahogany registration desk, with its background of hand-painted Mexican tile caused a momentary fear that perhaps he had gotten the wrong information from the travel agency. This place looked a little bit more expensive than he could afford.

He leaned on the counter. The well-manicured man standing behind it said, "May I help you, Sir?" There was a hint of an accent.

Bill looked quickly at his friends. "Do you have a reservation for Rutledge?"

The man flipped through a chart and beamed a smile back at him. "Yessir, Mr. Rutledge. Two rooms, each with two queen beds. You will be staying tonight and tomorrow. Perhaps one more day. Is that correct?"

Bill was embarrassed about the room situation. They hadn't really worked it out, but it had been agreed upon that two rooms was all they would rent. "Yes. That's right." He tossed his American Express card on the counter top. No sense using that thousand-dollar advance until he had to.

Bill stood, nervously looking at the ceiling and the corners of the room while the desk clerk ran his card through the machine and filled out the paperwork. He glanced from Tom to Connie, but avoided any chance of eye contact with Laura.

"Here you are, sir. Please sign right here." He

indicated a line on the form. "I already have the information provided to me by your travel agency." He laid two keys on the counter and said, "Your rooms are adjacent, rooms 114 and 115, on the northwest corner of the building." He looked at Laura and smiled. "It offers the most romantic and picturesque view in the building. If we may be of further assistance, please don't hesitate to call. My name is Frederico."

"Thanks, Frederico." Bill picked up the keys and walked quickly outside, the others tagging closely behind.

"Hey, Bill, you goin' to a fire?"

He stopped beside his car and handed Tom a key, then turned to Laura and gave her the other. "Look, I don't think this is going to work out this way." He looked at Connie and Tom. "I know you two are staying in the same room." He turned to Laura. "And I know there are two beds in the other room, but it still puts you at a disadvantage. I'll just go back in there and get another room. It's only forty or fifty bucks. I'm gonna be rollin' in dough here in a few days anyway."

Laura said nothing. Tom grabbed Bill by the sleeve as the latter turned to re-enter the lobby. "You haven't got the money yet, Bill. Laura's a big girl. I trust you with her."

"It ain't you I'm worried about trusting me, old buddy."

"Will you two quit it?" said Laura. "Bill, there's no need to spend another forty or fifty dollars a night just for a bed. If you're going to spend that kind of money, I'd just as soon you spent it on dinner. I'm not worried about you. You're probably the only friend Tom has who I don't worry about."

Bill looked at Tom quizzically. "I'm not sure if I was just complimented or insulted."

"I think it was meant as a big compliment, pal," said Tom with a sharp look at Laura.

"C'mon, you guys. Let's get our stuff to the rooms. I wanna get changed and go partying," said Connie as she moved to Tom's car.

The women used one room to shower and dress while the men used the other. Bill knew it was meant to make him feel more at ease, and he was grateful to Tom, who he knew was -- for him -- making the supreme sacrifice by not washing Connie's supple frame in a hot tub of water.

It was shortly after dark when they stepped outside and piled into Bill's GTO. The air was still comfortably warm so the top stayed down. Bill drove to the only restaurant in town he could remember.

It was a romantic little place down by the waterfront. Kerosene lamps dimly lighted the interior, with candles on each table. The food was excellent and the service, though casual, was superb. Their Mexican waiter spoke broken English but he knew his wines and his mixed drinks and suggested several wild concoctions for before dinner. Connie opted for something called "The Crazy Gringo". Tom joined her. Laura accepted a salty dog, and Bill stuck with his usual old fashioned.

Bill got over his uneasiness at the rooming arrangements and relaxed. The mood was at the same time festive and romantic. He remembered the one time he had been in this restaurant. For just a moment, he wished he hadn't brought these people here but then remembered how happy he had been then. *At least I had that time with her. She wouldn't mind. She'd understand.* He smiled sadly, absentmindedly.

"A penny for your thoughts."

He focused on Laura across the table. His heart jumped. *She said those same words to me that night.* "They aren't worth that much to anybody but me. Would you like another drink?"

I haven't even had one drink, and already she's the prettiest woman in town. Jesus, that hair is unreal!

Laura swirled her drink. "I'm fine. I think I'll nurse this one 'till dinner gets here."

Connie and Tom ordered another round and, before the second drink was finished, they were playing footsie under the table. Bill and Laura were saved the spectacle of more serious activity by the arrival of their meal.

After dining on spiced seafood and washing it down with Mexican beer, they left the restaurant in search of a nightclub. Based upon what Ernesto had told him, Bill had a pretty good idea of where to look. At an upscale club near the beach they stopped and parked the car to the loud brass sound of Mexican *mariachis* as it blasted into the night through the open front door. Bill raised the top on the Pontiac and locked the doors.

The place was dimly lit and smelled musty. Several people danced on a worn wooden floor surrounded by small tables. Larger booths lined the walls. They chose a booth in the shadows as near the dance floor as possible. Laura bumped him gently as she slid into the pink and black naugahyde booth.

"Sorry," she said.

"My pleasure," smiled Bill.

Connie and Tom strolled onto the dance floor before drinks were ordered, leaving him and Laura alone for the first time since they had arrived in town. He ordered a round of drinks, changing his own to bourbon and water. It would help to slow him down. This first night was not the night he expected to find his quarry but one never knows for sure, in the business of hunting fugitives, what the next moment will bring.

Laura looked exquisite in her light cotton dress. There was nothing particularly fancy about it. It was simple and moderately cut and the pale yellow accented her hair. *This gal's got class.*

"Do you dance?"

He looked at her. "Not very well until I've had a fifth, and then, still not too well, but by then I don't care."

"I guess what I've read about people like you is true, huh?"

"I dunno. What have you read?"

"That guys who play with guns aren't much in the romance department."

He looked up from his drink. *I guess I pegged this one wrong. Okay, lady, you asked for it.* "Is dancing the only form of romance you're talking about, or does your research delve into other areas?"

Laura put her hand to her lips. "Oh, my god. I just realized what that must have sounded like. I didn't mean it the way it came out." She pushed her drink away. "Maybe I've had too much to drink or something."

"Are you one of those people who use alcohol to excuse inexcusable behavior?" *Now why in the hell did I say that?*

"Look, Bill, I'm sorry. I don't know you well enough

to make those kinds of remarks. I guess... I don't know. I'm sorry. Will you accept my apology?"

He looked around the room. Julie Short and Michael Sturdivan were not here. He had studied their photos carefully. *Let's start over.* "I insist that I'm the one who owes the apology. I don't know what made me so thin-skinned all of a sudden. Who knows? Maybe what you say is true. Maybe I'm a lousy lover."

"I didn't say that."

"Well, whatever it was you said then." He pushed her drink to her. "Drink up. Who knows? We may both lighten up and say what we think without inhibitions." He downed his drink and placed the glass gently on the table. "What say we call a truce? We can say or ask whatever we want tonight without fear of reprisal and tomorrow we can go back to being hypocrites again."

She smiled and picked up her glass.

Bill ordered two more. *I'll start looking for Julie and Michael tomorrow. I rate a night of relaxation. As a matter-of-fact, I don't even care about those two tonight. I want to know about Ms. Laura O'whatever-it-was.*

Tom and Connie returned to the table, Connie all but seducing him between the dance floor and the booth.

"All right, you two, clean up your act until we get out of here. You're drawing more attention than the band," said Bill, half jokingly, half seriously. Connie would have drawn the attention from a blind man with her white cocktail dress. It was sleeveless and low-cut, and the short miniskirt was split almost to her hip on one side. There was no doubt in Bill's mind about her sex appeal. She had enough for a dozen women.

Laura seemed to sense his thoughts. "Connie is

pretty, isn't she?" She whispered in his ear.

He felt her hair brush against his cheek as she sat upright. He leaned into her ear and said. "No, she's not pretty, but she's one of the sexiest women this side of Shangri La. There's no denying that."

Laura pouted playfully.

Tom seemed to notice them for the first time since entering the club -- not that Bill could blame him. "Hey, what are you two being so secretive about?"

"Bill says Connie is the sexiest woman this side of Shangri La," said Laura playfully.

Bill shot her a quick sideward glance.

"Why, thank you, honey. You're not so bad yourself," purred Connie.

"Did he say that?" said Tom.

Bill rolled his eyes to the ceiling as he kicked Laura gently on the ankle.

"He did, and now he's kicking me under the table."

"Whatsamatter wi' you, Bill? You got your own gal." He eyed Laura up and down. "I'll grant you, she ain't no Raquel Welch, but she ain't half bad."

Bill felt Laura's leg brush his as she kicked Tom in the shin.

"Ow! Damnit, sis, that was too hard."

Bill snapped his head in her direction. "Sis? Did he call you sis?"

"Did he? He's called me so many things in the years I've known him, I hardly listen anymore."

"Are you his sister or not?"

She grinned. "Don't forget about our truce. After all, it was your idea."

"You're his sister?"

She said nothing.

"You *are* his sister. Why didn't you tell me? What's the big deal?"

Tom leaned over the table. "Take it easy, man. I was going to tell you."

"You? What about her?" He stared at Tom.

"It was my idea, Bill. I figured if you knew she was my sister, you might act differently than you would if you thought she was just another girl. I mean, hell, I haven't seen you go out for a long time." He gestured to Laura. "And Lorrie here just sits around her place and does nothing. I thought it would be good for both of you to get together."

"When were you going to tell me, Tom, old buddy -- before or after I made mad, passionate love to her?"

"Hey, that's my baby sister you're talking about."

"I thought she was just another girl."

"Now, damnit, Bill, you're starting to piss me off."

"You already did that for me. If I want to go out with someone, I'll ask for myself. The very least you should have done was told me she was your sister."

"And you wouldn't have wanted to go out with her. I know you."

Bill wanted to cuss him out, but his chauvinistic views held his tongue in check. "What difference would that have made to me?"

Tom shrugged. "I dunno. It just would've."

"Excuse me. Hey guys. Hey, you two. I'm sitting right here. If you don't mind, I'd appreciate it if you would stop talking about me like some inanimate object a thousand miles away."

Bill looked at her. "You stay out of this for a

minute." He turned back to Tom. "Of all the stupid things you've done in the time I've known you, this is about the stupidest. You force me on her, then you both set me up to think she's not who she is, and then…"

"Excuse me, gentlemen." Laura scooted to the outside of the booth and stood. She looked at Bill. "You're right. It was a lousy trick. So, if you'll excuse me, I'm going back to the room."

Bill scooted out the other side and stood. "No need, Red. Stay and have a good time. I'm outa here." He turned his back on them and walked out the door.

He was halfway across the street when he realized he had the keys to his car. He shrugged. *They'll catch a cab.* He smiled. *That damn Tom. Only he could have come up with something like this. I should have known she wasn't one of his bimbos. I'll call her when this thing is over.* He stepped into a bar.

This one was not one designed for the American tourist. The walls were stained concrete and the place smelled of old urine, stale beer and cigarette smoke. He picked a table near the end of the bar and sat on a chair with a wobbly leg. He had barely pulled his trouser legs down to cover his socks when a young prostitute sat next to him.

"American?"

He nodded.

"Buy me a drink?"

"Sure. What you having?"

She smiled and shouted to the bartender, then asked, "What you drink?"

"Bourbon and water. No, make that bourbon and soda."

He paid for the drinks and the girl moved next to him, rubbing her leg against his. "What your name?"

"Bill. What's yours?"

"Blanca." She leaned close and whispered. "You want a good time?"

He surveyed her closely. "Blanca, that sounds like a very tempting offer, but I have to be honest with you. I'm looking for my girlfriend."

"Such good-looking man like you can have more than one girlfriend." She ran her hand up his thigh. He grabbed it and held it gently.

"Blanca, I know you have to make a living, but I'm not the guy for you tonight. If you want to sit here and drink a few drinks with me, I'll buy them, but that's as far as it goes. If you can help me find my girl, I'll pay you whatever you normally charge for that other thing."

She giggled. "You funny gringo, Bill."

"Thanks."

"You have picture?"

"Sure." He reached into his shirt pocket and pulled out the two pictures that had been taken in the bondsman's office. He handed Julie Short's picture to her. "This is my girl. Her name is Julie. She may be using another name, but she's still the same ol' Julie."

Blanca took the picture and studied it. "Oow. She is *mui bonita* -- very pretty."

"Yeah, I know. And would you believe she's had three kids? Up and ran off with some hippie-looking dude about three months ago." He handed her the picture of Michael Sturdivan.

Her eyes grew wide and she glanced nervously around the room. "Are you sure this is the man she run away with?"

"Yes, I'm sure. Do you know him?"

She handed the pictures back to him under the table. "I know him."

Bill couldn't hold in his excitement. *Too much alcohol. Unprofessional.* He should have waited until tomorrow. "Where is he?"

She cast a quick glance around the room. "You come with me." She raised her voice slightly. "Only twenty dollars. I give you good time. C'mon. We go now." She stood.

Bill sat stupidly for a moment, then stood next to her. He whispered in her ear. "Why can't you tell me here?"

She giggled and pulled away. "No. No. You pay first. We not do anything in bar. We go to room."

Bill looked around. He felt the heat rise in his cheeks. "Okay. Okay. Let's go."

He followed her as she walked around the end of a bar and through a door that opened into a darkened hallway lined with rows of dirty doors. An old woman stood in the center of the hall. There was no expression on her face as he followed Blanca to one of the doors.

Blanca opened the door, stepped in, and motioned him inside. She closed the door behind him and locked it. The only light in the dingy room was provided by a bare forty-watt bulb hanging from the ceiling.

"Okay, what's this all about?" he whispered.

Blanca put her index finger to her lips, then began to undress.

"Hey, slow down. Whoa. You don't have to go through all of that. We'll just pretend that part. All I want is information on my girl."

"Shh. Get undressed. The old lady, she check you."

"The old lady -- she check me?"

"You know, V.D. She no check, she know something funny going on."

"You gotta be kidding?"

She shook her head. "No kidding. Get undressed."

He watched her unbutton her blouse to reveal two firm breasts, covered by a black lace bra. She nodded encouragement to him. "Hurry."

"Damn." Bill unbuttoned his sport shirt and put it on a small table. While Blanca was busy with her skirt, he quickly slipped the Walther PPK pistol and clip holster from his waistband and hid it under the shirt. When Blanca looked at him, he grinned and removed his trousers.

Bill stood in his under shorts with Blanca, who was clad only in black bra and panties. She opened the door and called the old woman, who entered the room almost immediately.

"Pull down your shorts," said Blanca. "She gotta check you out."

Bill grinned sheepishly. "Why didn't I think of that?" He pulled his shorts to his thighs.

The old woman gave him a cursory examination, peeling the foreskin on his penis back and checking for secretion. When she was satisfied, she nodded to Blanca.

"Pay her one dollar," said Blanca.

"Pay her one doll..." Bill reached for his trousers

and pulled a loose bill from one of the front pockets. He handed it to the old woman and she left the room, her face expressionless.

Bill looked at Blanca. He couldn't remember when he had ever felt so stupid. "Let's get down to business."

"You want good time?"

"All I want is information."

"That's okay. I no charge you anymore. Same price. You not bad looking." She smiled as she stared at the front of his shorts.

Bill turned around and picked his trousers from the small table. He put them on as Blanca giggled. She remained in bra and panties, even after he was completely dressed. "Why don't you put your clothes back on?"

"Not yet. What happen if I have to open door for old woman? She think something funny going on if I have clothes on and we still in room. Whatsamatter? You 'fraid you might change mind -- want good time?"

"No," he smiled. "You're pretty and all that, but I love my girl. Now what can you tell me?" The Walther felt good resting in the small of his back.

She held out her hand and wiggled her fingers. He dropped a twenty-dollar bill into it. She stuffed it into her cleavage and sat on the old steel bed. "I know the one you call Michael, but I hope your girlfriend not mixed up with him."

"Where can I find him?"

"I don't know where he live, but he come see me alla time."

"He does?"

"Alla time. I think maybe your girlfriend not with

him or her pussy no good."

Bill stifled a giggle. "Well, our relationship was more than just sex."

"I hope so."

"How often does this Michael guy come to see you?"

"Every night."

"Every night?"

"That's what I say. Every night."

"Has he been here yet tonight?"

She smiled, showing two rows of perfect white pearls. "No, but he come soon."

"Blanca, don't tell him I'm looking for him."

"You let him have good time with Blanca?"

He looked her up and down and laughed softly. "I wouldn't deprive any man of that pleasure." He handed her another twenty. "This is not to say anything."

She snatched the money. "I not say nothing." She put her clothes on and said, "We go now, okay?"

"Okay. You lead the way." He followed her out of the room, down the hall and back into the bar. As they stepped back into the cantina, he saw Laura about the same time she saw him. She was sitting alone, sipping a margarita, looking every bit the lost soul in search of someone. *Oh, Christ.*

CHAPTER 5

The look on Laura's face was first one of shock, then disbelief, then anger. Bill glanced at Blanca, then at Laura. He smiled weakly at Laura as she stared up at him from her table.

"Next time you want good time, you see me, okay?" said Blanca as she sat at the empty table next to Laura's.

Great. This is going to be good. He nodded and walked past Laura's table, toward the door facing the street.

"Do you remember me, Mister?" said Laura.

I knew it wouldn't work, but I had to give it a try. He turned slowly and faced her. "Laura, I can't explain now. Let it go for awhile," he said softly.

"What's there to explain? I don't care what you do. You're a grown man, and I certainly don't have any right to tell you what to do, but I did expect you to say hello." She looked over at Blanca. "But now that I think about it, I guess you did the right thing by ignoring me." She looked near tears.

He walked back to her table. "May I sit down?" he said softly.

She looked into his eyes. "I don't care what you do, Bill Rutledge. That's the truth. I just don't care." A tear trickled down her cheek.

He sat and scooted the chair close to her. "Please, listen. I promise there's an explanation for this, and it isn't what you think." He raised his voice. "Can I buy you a drink?" He glanced at Blanca staring at him curiously, then whispered, "That girl can't know that you came here with me."

The look on her face was one of incredulousness. She wiped a wet eye. "You don't have to worry about that, because I'm *not* with you." She looked at the ceiling. "I don't believe this," she said to no one. "I don't believe this. What am I doing here?"

Out of the corner of his eye, Bill noticed a man enter the cantina. He turned and saw Michael Sturdivan. His heart thumped in his chest. He turned back to Laura. "Laura, I don't have time to explain."

"I still don't know what I'm doing here." She leaned forward and stared into his eyes. "Maybe you can tell me."

Two men in a dark corner of the bar stood. Bill saw the pistols come out from under the sport shirts. "Not now!" He pushed Laura hard in the chest, sending her reeling to the floor, at the same time reaching for his Walther PPK. He heard a woman screaming. One of the men in the corner fired a shot. It whizzed past Bill's head, toward the door and his bounty.

"No!" He fired into the dark corner. The man who fired the first shot fell back into the wall. The other fired wildly in Bill's direction, forgetting about his original target. Bill cranked off three quick rounds and the man fell over the table, sending the two beer bottles there crashing to the floor.

Bill glanced quickly around the room. Everyone was out of sight -- behind the bar or under tables. Laura lay flat on her back, the way she had landed. "Get up and get out of here, lady!"

She struggled to her feet, rubbing her chest. "What about you?"

"Get the hell out of here!" His eyes panned the room, waiting for movement. Laura rushed out through the door. Bill turned to the table nearest the door. Michael Sturdivan crouched under it, unmoving.

Bill waved his pistol at him. "Get up, Mike. You and me are gettin' the hell outa here."

"Who the hell are you?" He didn't move.

"It looks like I'm the guy who just saved your bacon from somebody who wants you dead. Now get up before I change my mind and finish their job."

"Who the hell are you?" Still he didn't move.

Bill kicked the table hard, knocking it over. "Get up, goddamnit, before I blow your brains out! We gotta get the hell outa here before the police get here."

"Okay, okay. Lighten up, dude. Don't wave that fucking pistol in my face. It might go off or something -- you know what I mean?"

"Shut up and get up. Out the door. C'mon, let's go." Bill grabbed him by an arm, jerked him to his feet and, with a shove, sent him through the open door. Outside, he motioned to Sturdivan. "Stay right by my side. If it looks like you're gonna get lost, I'll waste you. Got it?"

"Yeah, man, I got it. What the fuck is this, some kind of rip off? If it is, man, you fucked up. I don't have any…"

"Shut up!" He jerked Sturdivan into an alley, searching for a glimpse of Laura before he lost view of the street, but she was nowhere to be seen.

They ran several blocks, turning and backtracking and turning again. Finally, out of breath and exhausted, they stopped in a dark alley and hid among several trashcans. When he had recovered enough to speak, Bill said. "Ev'nin', Mike." He drew one more deep breath. "I'm Bill Rutledge, private investigator, and you, my friend, are under arrest."

"Are you crazy? What the hell have you been smokin'? You don't have any authority down here."

"Shh. Keep your voice down before I cut your tongue out." He waved the Walther in front of Sturdivan's face. "For now, this is my authority."

"It works for me, man. Okay, okay, so I'm under arrest. What the hell you gonna do now -- march me back to the border?"

"Not just yet. We gotta pick up a friend of yours on the way out."

"What friend? I don't know anybody down here."

"You know, Mike, I'm beginning to like your sense of humor, but the truth is, I don't have time for it yet. Maybe later, okay? Now, where is Julie?"

Sturdivan looked absentmindedly at the wall next to them. "Julie? Julie. Let me see. There was a Julie in my seventh grade math class. Oh, yeah, there was another Julie my freshman..."

Bill jammed the Walther into Sturdivan's throat and pushed hard, choking off his voice. "You're worth just as much to me dead as you are alive. And It'll be a lot easier to find her if I don't have to drag your ass around, so I'm not gonna waste any more time. You gonna tell me where she is, or do I waste you and cut off a hand? The prints will identify you."

Sturdivan gagged and coughed. Bill pulled the pistol away from his throat. Sturdivan looked at him with a new kind of look, one of total fear. "Jesus! You're crazy, man," he rasped.

Bill grinned. "Yeah, I know. How do you want it? Sorry we don't have time for the last cigarette bit, but you do understand that I'm in a hurry, right?"

Sturdivan's eyes were round with horror. "Shit, man, let her be. She hasn't done anything."

"Yeah, I know. And neither have you, but that doesn't make any difference. You're both worth a hundred thousand apiece to me, and you're both goin' back to the States. All of you, or pieces -- I don't really care which way you want it." He cocked the hammer on the double-action Walther.

"Wait! I'll show you where she is, you low-life bastard."

Bill un-cocked the pistol and smiled. "Now that's a little better. I think I see an improvement in your attitude."

"Fuck you."

"Sorry, Mike, you're not my type." He stood. "C'mon. Let's go."

Three blocks from where they had hidden among the garbage cans, Sturdivan stopped outside a plastered adobe apartment building. "Ground floor -- apartment 104."

"You wouldn't try to set me up, would you, Mike?"

He shook his head. "No way. I believe you're crazy enough to kill me."

"You're not as dumb as you look, Mike." He glanced around them. "Come with me." He led Sturdivan to a wrought-iron gate on the south end of the apartment building and withdrew a pair of handcuffs from his back pocket.

"Oh no. You can't do this to me, man. What if those people try to get me again tonight -- while you're getting Julie?"

"Hell, Mike, I'll only be gone a few minutes. You'll be all right." He cuffed him to the gate and turned to leave.

"Hey, man, it's apartment 103."

Bill smiled. "Are you sure this time?"

Sturdivan looked at his feet. "I thought it would be funny if you barged in on Pedro. He's a big, burly fisherman. I thought it'd be real funny to see him whip your ass."

Bill clucked. "Shame on you, Mike. Just when I was beginning to like you too. Back in a few minutes." He turned and walked back to the center of the building where the hall door was located.

He walked down the dimly lit hall until he stood next to the door marked with the number 103. When he tried the doorknob, it turned easily and the door came open slightly. He eased it slowly open and peeked into the apartment.

A soft light burned in the corner of the combination kitchen and living room. An unattended stereo, nestled in an expensive cabinet, played classical music. Bill's heart pounded in his ears. He held his breath and listened for movement. There was none. He stepped inside the apartment and quietly closed the door behind him. A light burned in the bedroom. He pulled out his pistol and went through the door in a low crouch. It was empty. *Shit!*

The sound of the front door opening sent him flat against the wall in the bedroom. The refrigerator door opened and closed, then there was the sound of a pop-top on a can. A pair of shoes hit the floor and a large beanbag was reshaped. *There's only one of them.*

Bill stepped into the doorway and pointed his pistol at Julie Short. He had her picture with him, and he was sure he had the right person, but the picture did her no justice. She sat on the beanbag, her long tanned legs stretched to the limit, the cut-off jeans hiding almost none of them, her white cotton blouse unbuttoned and tied in a knot at the bottom. Long blonde hair hung to the floor behind her. He almost forgot why he was there.

Her large blue eyes grew larger as they squared off with his. Quickly, she glanced at the door, then back to him. A resigned look overtook her face. "You want a beer?"

Bill put his right hand out, palm upward. "Up, Julie. We haven't got much time. Mike's waitin' for us outside."

"You going to shoot me with that thing or what?" She was outwardly calm.

"I don't know. That's up to you. You gonna get up, or do I beat you to death and drag you with me anyway?"

"What do you want? Money? Sex? Drugs? What?"

"I want your little body in jail in Los Angeles, California. Now get up."

He thought he saw fear in her eyes. "You a cop? You got no jurisdiction down here."

"I'm a private investigator. This is all the

jurisdiction I need right now." He waved the pistol.

"You'll have to use your jurisdiction then, mister, because I'm not going back to L.A. with you or anybody else." She sat stiffly in the beanbag.

Damn! Now what? His other set of cuffs was in the GTO. He leaned over and grabbed her arm. She resisted stiffly for a second then went limp and kicked him swiftly in the groin. "Ow!" He stuffed the pistol in his waistband and wrestled her to the floor, his stomach turning from the pain. He pinned her with his body and held her arms with his own while he waited for the pain to leave him.

"Are you having fun, you sonofabitch?" Her breath was hot in his ear.

"Just shut up a second." His voice was hoarse. When the pain subsided enough for him to regain his sensory perception, he felt the contours of her body against his. He smelled the sweet odor of her perspiration. "Don't do anything that stupid again." Quickly he was on his feet and jerking her to hers. He pulled her hands behind her back and held them there while he searched for something to tie them with. He found a ball of twine and dragged her to the kitchen counter where it sat.

"I'm gonna tie your hands. So help me, if you make one move, I'll kill you, you understand?"

She nodded. "Okay, big shot. You win for now, but it's a long way from here to the border."

He tied her quickly, using several strands of the twine to complete the job satisfactorily. When he was finished, he showed her the ball of twine and said, "You guys should use better quality twine for shipping the kind of stuff you deal in."

She curled a lip. "You're so damn smart. You don't know the first thing about me or Mike."

"I know you're both wanted, and I know I've got you both. That's all I have to know about you. Now just be real quiet, and we'll get out of here without anyone getting hurt."

"I want to see Mike."

"You will if you keep your mouth shut. One peep out of you and you won't wake up for a week. Understand?"

"Big man. Got me all tied up. Gonna put me in chains now and get real kinky?"

"Shut up." He grabbed the front of her blouse and she jumped back, eyes wide with fear. "Hold still, damnit. I'm gonna button this blouse. You'll get enough attention without this added attraction. His fingers shook as he tried to accomplish the task quickly.

The fear in her eyes disappeared and a smile spread across her lips. "You aren't such a bad-ass after all, are you? Are you one of those puritan types, like Magnum P.I. or something like that?" She laughed. "For crying out loud, you can't even button up a blouse right."

He continued to button the blouse up to the bottom of her neck. "I've never seen any need to button up a lady's blouse. My area of expertise is how to unbutton one." He smiled.

"Hey, don't you think you went a little overboard? I can't breath in this heat with this thing buttoned up that high."

Deftly, Bill reached up and unbuttoned the top two buttons in one smooth movement. "Can you live with that?"

She smiled smartly. "If you can, I can."

Bill shook his head. "C'mon, we're gettin' outa here." He held her arm above the elbow as they stepped onto the old cracked sidewalk and located Sturdivan handcuffed to the wrought-iron gate at the end of the building. Julie jerked her arm from his grip and stared at him, daring him to hold her arm again. Bill shrugged. "I just took a shower, and I don't want to have to touch you anymore than I have to. I'm not doing it for my health. It's you I'm worried about. You run and I shoot -- understand?"

"I don't believe you'd shoot an unarmed woman."

The dim glow from a distant street lamp cast enough light for her to see his smile, of that he was certain. "Not only will I shoot an unarmed woman, but I'll shoot her in the back."

Sturdivan jerked his cuffs against the gate. "He means it, Julie. He's crazier'n hell. He just wasted two guys down at the Cabana Club."

She looked at Bill, more than a little fear showing on her face. Quickly she forgot her fear and looked at Sturdivan. "The Cabana Club? What were you doing at the Cabana Club?"

Bill stepped between them. "I hate to break up this lover's spat, but until I get you Stateside, you're on my time." He uncuffed one of Sturdivan's hands long enough to unhook him from the gate, then re-cuffed him with his hands behind his back.

Sturdivan looked at him threateningly. "You know, you can be a real pain in the ass, man."

"Thanks. Now, be quiet and let's get moving."

"Where we going?" asked Sturdivan.

"I've got a car parked by a restaurant."

Julie looked at Sturdivan and shrugged. "At least he isn't going to make us walk."

"You think this is funny?" asked Sturdivan.

"No -- do you?" She shot back.

"I said keep it quiet." Bill walked between them, hands on their elbows.

The GTO sat quietly in a dark section of the center of the block, the light from the street lamps on the corners not quite reaching that far. The top was up and the car locked. He cuffed both prisoners to the passenger door handle while he unlocked the driver's side, then left Sturdivan cuffed to the door while he put Julie in the back seat and retrieved his other cuffs and retaining straps and chained her to the chromed metal bar he had welded to the side panel.

Sturdivan he cuffed and strapped to the chromed bar where his glove compartment had been. "Jesus Christ, man -- what kind of a fucking car is this?"

Bill started the engine. The throaty rumble of the Ram Air IV engine vibrated the chassis. He smiled. "It's my 'bring 'em back alive or maybe dead' car."

"Funny. Real fucking funny."

"You asked." He pushed in the clutch, put the transmission into first gear and lifted his foot slowly, letting the big engine pull the car from a stop without using the accelerator. He shifted gears slowly and at low engine rpm so as not to attract any attention from whoever might still be on the streets. He turned onto the main highway north and accelerated to a comfortable seventy miles an hour. He reached over and slapped Sturdivan in the mouth.

"Ow! What the hell was that for?"

"Watch your language," replied Bill.

"We gonna stop and eat?" asked Sturdivan.

"No need." Bill reached under his seat and withdrew a large brown paper bag. "You want a sandwich?"

CHAPTER 6

A three-quarter moon hung low on the horizon as Bill pulled the GTO to the side of the road and shut off the engine. They had been driving only thirty minutes.

"What the fuck are you doing?"

Bill turned to face him, the moon casting a silvery glow on his face and accenting the shadows of his cheekbones. He reached out and slapped Sturdivan solidly on the cheek.

"Ow! Jesus Christ, what the hell was that for? Take these cuffs offa me, you asshole and try that shit again." Sturdivan jerked his cuffs roughly against the bar.

Bill grabbed him by the front of his shirt. "That, my friend, was for your foul mouth. You can talk like you want in front of your mother, but while you're my prisoner, and while we're in the company of a female, you *will* clean up your act -- you got it?"

Sturdivan half laughed. "That's real fucking rich, man. You think she hasn't heard it before?"

Bill slapped him again. "That's not the question. The question is, 'is she gonna continue to hear it now?' If so, your face is gonna look like hamburger before we hit the States."

Sturdivan fought his cuffs and jerked them violently in an attempt to pull the bar loose from the dash.

"Quit trying to tear my car up."

"What's the matter, big shot? You afraid I might get loose and whip your ass?"

Bill sighed and reached into his pocket. He pulled out his handcuff key. "I could just shoot you and this would be a lot simpler, but I guess I'd rather beat you to death now that I think about it." He put the key into one of the cuffs.

Sturdivan held still and watched him closely. "You're really gonna do it?"

Bill nodded, "You bet I am. The thought of listening to your mouth all the way to LA doesn't appeal to me."

Sturdivan looked at Julie in the back seat. She watched interestedly, but said nothing. He looked back at Bill. "You're gonna shoot me as an escaping prisoner, right?"

Bill unlocked one of the cuffs. Sturdivan didn't move. His face had a worried look. "Lock it back on, man. I'm not going for the old 'escaped prisoner trick.' You can forget about that one. Lock it, man. I ain't movin'."

Bill snapped the cuff back onto Sturdivan's wrist. "Yeah, I guess you're just too smart for me, Mike, ol' boy."

Mike stared at him. "You were really gonna make a fight of it, weren't you?"

"We'll never know now, will we? You passed up your chance to find out."

"What the hell kind of a person are you? You chase people down for a living, then you get mad because they cuss in front of a woman -- and the woman is a prisoner too. You shoot people you don't even know and run from the police -- the Mexican police anyway -- and you break more laws in one night than I do in a year.

You're crazy, man. You got your priorities fu -- screwed up."

"I always did have, Mike -- always did have." He reached under the driver's seat and withdrew a steel thermos. "This is the real reason I stopped. Would you guys like some coffee?"

Mike looked at Julie. "I don't believe this guy," he said with a nod of his head in Bill's direction.

"I'll have some," she said, then looked at Mike. "We might as well get it while it's being offered."

"Yeah, I guess I could use a cup of coffee. Since it don't look like you're gonna offer us any booze," said Mike.

"Oh, you'd rather have a shot of bourbon?" Bill reached under the passenger seat and withdrew a pint of bourbon.

"I'll just be damned," said Mike. "You got any other surprises?"

Bill winked. "If I told you, then they wouldn't be surprises anymore."

"Never mind. I'll take a shot of that whiskey now."

Bill held the pint to Mike's lips while the latter gulped the whiskey thirstily. "Whoa. Take it easy there, Mike. We got a long way to go."

He pulled the bottle down and offered it to Julie. She shook her head. "I'll take the coffee. I don't trust any man that offers a handcuffed woman a drink."

Bill grinned and took a small swig. "I hadn't thought of that, but don't flatter yourself. You're my prisoner and nothing else." He put the whiskey bottle back in its place and poured coffee into the thermos cap. He sat the cup on the dash and turned to Julie. "I'm going to un-cuff one of your hands. Don't do anything stupid like trying to throw it on me. If you do that, I'll empty the thermos on you. Do we understand each other?"

She nodded. "Just give me the coffee. I don't need a lecture."

He handed her the cup and stepped out of the car into the cool night air. His hands shook as he lit a cigarette. Mike was at least twenty pounds heavier than him, and apparently in good shape. He had almost risked two hundred thousand dollars. He would have fought him one-on-one had Mike not been suspicious and backed out. *Why?*

"Hey, mister bounty hunter, can I have one of those?"

Bill leaned in the window and handed his smoke to Julie. "I'm not unlocking two of you at the same time. You give him a hit when he wants it."

Julie sat the coffee cup on the floorboard and accepted the cigarette silently. She held it to Mike's lips while Bill lit another for himself. When he finished, he fieldstripped the butt, re-cuffed both of Julie's hands, and got back into the car. With the cap on the thermos, and it safely tucked under his seat, Bill started the car and continued north.

The engine was its usual, dependable self. Bill felt good. Everything had gone much better than he had expected. He hadn't planned on locating Mike and Julie for another day or two if he was lucky. The two men in the bar concerned him, but they had been shooting at his bounty, and Bill couldn't allow that. He wondered if they were dead or alive. Of course, it wouldn't really matter as far as the Mexican law was concerned. He would get ten years just for carrying the Walther. In a Mexican jail, that generally meant life.

He continued to watch the road ahead as he spoke. "Hey, Mike, who were those guys trying to blow your brains out?"

Mike shrugged. "I dunno, man. Probably just some people I piss -- er irritated a while ago."

"When you irritate someone, you really do it right."

"You know who they are," said Julie suddenly.

"Stay out of this. Let's leave it alone, okay?"

"No. Not okay. They're going to get us, Mike. It won't matter if we're in the States or not." She nodded at Bill. "They'll go through this guy like Sherman went through Georgia."

"I take offense to that," muttered Bill.

"It doesn't really matter what you take offense to, mister bounty hunter. These guys are pros. They'll take you out in a New York minute," she said.

"I don't take out all that easy, lady, and as long as I'm alive, nobody is taking you or Mike out either. You sure aren't showing much faith. I'm kinda disappointed."

"You think that little pea shooter is gong to stop them?" she asked.

"If you're referring to my PPK, I'll remind you that it did a fair job of gettin' Mike here out of some pretty serious trouble."

"Look, man, if it's money you want, why don't you let us go? I've got money stashed. You said we were worth two hundred thousand. I'll give you an even quarter of a million -- cash."

Bill took his eyes off the road momentarily and looked at Mike. "You know, that's probably the most lucrative money offer I've ever heard."

"But you're not going to take it, right?" said Julie from the back seat.

Bill smiled. "See, you're beginning to know me better already."

"Shit."

"Hey, man, how come you didn't smack her in the mouth for cussin'?" asked Mike.

"I don't hit ladies."

"What a bunch of fucking shit."

Bill backhanded Mike across the mouth.

"Ow! Hey, man, that hurt."

"The rules haven't changed."

"When I get loose, you'll see how much the rules have changed."

"Sorry, Mike, you ain't gettin' loose. That's a pipe dream."

"Look, mister bounty hunter, these people are going to kill us. You can't stop them. If we'd known they knew where we were, we'd have been gone," said Julie, a pleading tone creeping into her voice. "Take our money and let us go. Why go through all of this for less money than we're offering?"

"Sorry, Julie -- I don't deal with bounties."

"That's stupid. What's it going to get you -- a note on your tombstone -- 'Here lies the bounty hunter -- he didn't make deals with bounties'? That's real brave and stupid of you, mister bounty hunter."

"I appreciate you adding the 'brave' part."

Julie sat silently, brooding.

"How much farther to Nogales?" asked Mike.

"We should be running up on Imuris in a little bit.

From there it's about thirty minutes to the border."

Mike sat in silence for a moment. "I can't believe we got this far. So what happens when we get into the States?"

"I take you to LA -- what do you think?"

"C'mon, man, lighten up. Give us a break. I'm serious -- we're dead meat if you put us back in jail."

"I don't think you're as important as you think you are. I haven't seen any hoods with guns chasing us."

"They don't know who you are, or what you're driving, but once they figure it out, they'll find us."

"To tell you the truth, I'm more worried about the police than I am your friends."

"I gotta go to the bathroom," said Julie.

"Great. Okay, hang on until we get to Imuris. I'll figure something out."

"It better be fast."

The lights of Imuris peaked over the top of a hill. Bill pushed down a little harder on the accelerator and the GTO responded with a quick burst to ninety miles an hour.

"Hey, she don't have to go that bad, man."

"Relax, Mike. It's not a bad road, and we've got four lanes to roll around on."

Mike held his silence as the lights of Imuris grew brighter.

Bill pulled the GTO into the only all night service station in town. It wasn't a service station really; more like a small store with a gas pump and dirty restrooms.

He unlocked Julie from the car and led her to the women's room. He searched for a place to cuff her wrist to something solid but found nothing. Julie tapped her foot. "Look, this is getting serious. I'm not going anywhere. There's only one door. Just give me thirty seconds. As a matter-of-fact, you can stand here and watch if you want. I've got to go."

Bill let go of the opened cuff. "I'll be right outside the door."

She smiled. "You're weird as hell, you know that?"

He looked at her tanned legs in the light cast by the bare bulb overhead. "Yeah, I know." He stepped outside and lit a cigarette. He listened to the splashing sounds in the toilet inside the restroom. When it stopped, he waited ten seconds and stepped inside. "You better be ready, 'cause here I am."

The buttons on her blouse were undone again, the garment held together only by the knot at the bottom. "I thought I told you to keep that thing buttoned up."

"What's the matter, mister bounty hunter -- can't take it?"

"I can take it all right. And I can leave it. Now button it up before I sew it up to your neckline."

She moved close to him and put her body against his. "C'mon. Let's you and me make it right here. There won't be many chances for me where you're taking me -- unless you find it so good you decide to change your mind and take me and the money both."

Deftly, he pulled up her hands and cuffed them together. He reached for the front of her blouse and buttoned it up until he ran out of buttons. He was less self-conscious this time. "This is getting to be a regular habit with us, you know that?"

"You sonofabitch."

"You never met my mother."

"You passed up the best offer you'll ever have."

He looked her over from head to toe and grinned. "You know, you just might be worth the whole two-hundred thousand -- but I don't deal with bounties. Besides, it wouldn't be fair to Mike. He seems like such a nice guy." He pushed her gently by him and out the door.

"You sonofabitch. Quit pushing me around."

When he opened the driver's door and folded it forward to allow her entry, Mike glanced up at her buttoned blouse. "I see he didn't go for the gusto." He looked at Bill. "Mister, you must be a hard man to please."

"Shut up," said Julie as she stepped into the back of the car.

"I'm getting hungry," said Mike.

Bill looked at the old woman sleeping in a chair inside the store. "I hate to wake her, but I guess it's for a good cause." He locked Julie's cuffs in place and walked into the store.

The woman continued to sleep while he picked up potato chips and candy bars and three bottles of soda pop. He banged the bottles on the counter discreetly and the old woman nodded her head, looked up at him, then slowly got to her feet. "*Es todo?*"

"*Si.*" He put a ten-dollar bill on the chipped Formica counter top.

She looked at the bill and counted change from a paper bag into his hands. It was in pesos. Bill stuffed the Mexican money into his pocket without counting it and stepped outside. He glanced to the east. The sun would be rising soon.

He sat in the GTO and shared the food with his prisoners.

"You call this food? I'll bet you really know how to treat a girl on a date," said Julie.

"Depends on the girl. I don't think you'd like the other choices in there."

She took a bite of a Hershey bar. "I forgive you this time, but I want champagne and caviar next time."

Bill thought of Laura. "I think my kind of girl would want a good red wine and Chateaubriand."

"That's not a bad idea either. Maybe there's still hope for you yet," said Julie

"Look, man," said Mike around a mouthful of potato chips. "You ain't such a bad guy. I'll make it an even three-hundred thousand and you let us go."

"Not a chance," said Bill without hesitation.

"Hey, mister bounty hunter, what did you do before you hunted people down like rats for a living?" asked Julie.

"I was just a normal hard-working businessman, like a lot of other hard-working businessmen."

"What kind of business?"

"I tried a few: a racing shop, a tool and die shop -- I even tried my hand at making computers."

"No kidding? What happened?"

"The racing business died. I sold my tool and die shop for a nice profit, and I was too far ahead of my time with the thought that someday computers would be like television sets -- everybody would own one -- and I couldn't survive until the rest of the country caught up with me. What did you do before you started dealing in dope?"

"I've never dealt dope."

"The DA in Los Angeles seems to think he's got a pretty good case against you from what I read."

"It's a frame, man!" said Mike.

"Yeah. Okay, it's a frame."

"He's telling it straight," said Julie.

"For a man who doesn't seem to be gainfully employed, he sure seems to have a lot of dough. How'd he get it -- win the Mexican lottery?"

"Screw you, mister bounty hunter," said Julie.

"You tried that once, I believe."

"It's not from dealing, man," said Mike.

"Then what?"

Mike hesitated. "We ripped off a big drug deal going down in Mazatlan. It's drug money, but all we did was take it from the dealers. We didn't sell any dope, man."

"You ripped off one of the big boys?"

Mike nodded. "Carrerra."

"Chuy Carrerra?"

"That's the one."

"You'd a been better off kissing a cobra."

"Now do you believe me when I say these guys are gonna get us?"

Bill started the car. "Maybe. But not while you're in my custody." He released the clutch and pulled back onto the highway.

Bill saw the lights about two miles north of Imuris. The flashing blue lights had been hidden by a small hill. He was within a quarter of a mile before he stopped the car.

"Now what, mister bounty hunter?"

He shot a glance at Julie in the back seat. "We'll try to talk our way through 'em."

"Fat chance. They've seen you stop. They'll know

something is up," said Mike.

"Good point, Mike. What do you suggest?"

"Let's go back to Guaymas. I've got connections there. I'll have us out of the country in a few hours."

"Bad idea, Mike. We'll go back to Imuris and head east toward Agua Prieta or Naco." A shiver ran up his spine. Just the thought of Naco made him shake. He turned the GTO around and started back to Imuris.

Suddenly the sharp crack of gunfire reached his ears. Bill looked in the rear-view mirror and saw a set of headlights following them at a high rate of speed. *Shit!* "Hang on tight."

"What the hell are you doing? Are you crazy? There's probably a hundred of 'em south of here by now. You can't run into 'em at ninety miles an hour," shouted Mike over the roar of the engine.

"Shut up. I'm thinking."

"He's thinking. He's goddamn thinking!" shouted Mike to no one in particular.

Bill reached over and backhanded him in the mouth. "This doesn't change the rules."

"Ow!"

A bullet slammed into the side view mirror on the driver's side. "Damn! That does it." Bill slammed on the brakes and turned the wheel sharply to the left. Just as the car started to slide sideways, he downshifted into low gear and punched the accelerator pedal to the floor. The rear tires broke traction and spun the rear of the car around. When they were facing the charging police vehicle, Bill came off the accelerator and turned the wheel sharply to the right, just enough to let the car straighten itself.

"Jesus! What the hell are you doing?" screamed Julie.

"You're fucking crazy, man!" shouted Mike.

Bill reached out and slapped Mike in the mouth again.

"Ow!"

"Oh, shit! He's driving right at them!" shouted Julie.

CHAPTER 7

The smell of burning rubber hung in the air like cordite over a battlefield. Bill held the accelerator to the floor as he reached up under the dash and withdrew a stainless steel Smith and Wesson .357 magnum revolver. As the distance between the two vehicles closed rapidly, he leaned out the window and fired at the area between the approaching headlights. The police car swerved and rolled into a ditch on the side of the road, disappearing in a cloud of dust. Bill hit the brakes and repeated his earlier turn, heading south for Imuris.

"Is everybody all right?"

"Is everybody all right! What the hell kind of question is that?" shouted Mike. "You just tried to get us all killed."

"It doesn't appear I was very successful. Your mouth is still alive. How about you back there?"

"Where in the hell did you ever learn to drive like that?"

"I was a cop once. First in my class on the pursuit driving course."

""What about the shooting? How can you shoot from a moving car and hit a tire?"

"I was aiming for the radiator."

Bill slowed the car down and threw the transmission into neutral.

"Now what the hell are you doing?" asked Mike.

"If we get by the old lady without waking her up, they might not know we went east until we're home free." They coasted passed the little store and turned left at the junction of Highway 2. Only when they had almost stopped rolling did Bill put the car into gear and resume their flight.

"How much other shit you got hidden in this car?" asked Mike.

Bill slapped him.

"Ow!"

Bill shook his head. "If you live long enough, you'll learn to clean up your mouth."

The sun was peeking over the Sierra Madre Occidental range when Bill pulled the car to a stop. He unhooked the top and lowered it.

"Hey, man, what's this all about?" asked Mike.

"I don't think they know this is a convertible. When we go through Cananea, we're gonna have to stop for gas. When we stop, we're gonna be three tourists, you got it?"

"Sure, I got it. I always go touring in my handcuffs."

"We're gonna make a few changes. Julie is getting in the front seat with us. I'm going to un-cuff you both, but I'll have this Smith in my left hand all the time -- and it's like I told you earlier -- I get my money whether you're dead or alive, so have it your way."

"Oh boy, I get to sit up front with the grown ups." Julie quipped.

Bill un-cuffed Julie and sat her on the edge of the bucket seat on the passenger side, then he moved around to Mike and uncuffed him, tucking both sets of cuffs into his waistband at his back, next to the Walther.

When he sat behind the wheel, Julie moved close to him, straddling the empty space between the seats. She picked up her left foot and put it on the driver's side of the floor shifter, rubbing her leg against his, a smile on her lips. "Don't you just love a convertible? I think they're so romantic."

"Save your act for Cananea. You may need it there."

"How far is it?" she cooed.

"Just a few minutes I think."

"I'll try to be good that long." She placed her head on his shoulder.

He shrugged it off. "Julie, this is serious. I'm taking you in and that's all there is to it. The only way it won't happen is if you get us all killed. I'll guarantee you if I go, I'm taking you both with me."

She sat up straight, a mock grin on her face. "Yes sir! Will that be all, sir, or would you like to beat me before we continue? Jesus, I just thought you might lighten up a little."

Bill started the engine and roared back onto the two-lane highway. The wind felt good in his face. He hadn't realized how tired he was getting. A few hours sleep would be nice.

Cananea was a good-sized town for this part of Mexico. It even had its own little airport, which was one of the reasons it was as large as it was. From Cananea, it was only a short distance by air to the U.S. border and a night airdrop. At certain times of the year, the population of the town could double, depending upon the size of the marijuana crops in the south.

Bill pulled into a semi-modern gas station and put his arm around Julie's shoulders.

"Uhm. That feels good." She wiggled against him.

"Be quiet," said Bill softly out of the corner of his mouth.

A middle-aged man stepped out of the lube bay, wiping his hands on a rag. *Buenos dias.* You want gasoline?"

"Fill it."

He moved to the rear of the car, lifted the license plate and removed the gas cap.

"I think this guy's stolen this kind of car before," said Mike. "He knew right where the gas cap was."

"They were in high demand in their day," answered Bill.

"You must have been in high demand in your day too, huh?" said Julie.

Bill turned and looked her in the eye. "I hope you do as well."

She raised an eyebrow. "Oow, a real lover boy, huh?" She rubbed her bare leg against his trousers.

"Cool it, or I'll pistol whip you right here in front of Mike and the rest of the population of Mexico."

She pouted. "It's hard to believe you've ever been anything but a hard ass."

"You keep talking like that and I'm going to forget Mike's lessons and let him go back to talking like a bum."

She glanced at Mike. "We can't have that now, can we?" She turned back to Bill. "I forgot for a second there that I was a lady. I thought I was a captured fugitive, and everybody knows how captured fugitives talk."

Bill opened his door. Out of the side of his mouth he said, "Don't move, I'm gonna check the oil."

Bill quickly checked the oil and, by peeking under the hood, was able to maintain eye contact with Mike and Julie. He couldn't afford to take a chance with his car, especially not now. He closed the hood just as Mike opened his door.

"Where do you think you're going?"

"They've found us, man."

"What are you talking about?"

Mike pointed frantically at a telephone booth. "That fucker is one of them."

"Get back in the car -- now!" said Bill softly but forcefully.

Mike jumped back into the passenger seat and sat low. Julie was hunkered down with him. Bill sat calmly behind the wheel, his hands trembling as he felt the Smith and Wesson on his left hip, the Walther tucked into his waist band at the small of his back. The attendant approached, the rag still in his hands. Bill swung the door open and stepped out of the car, the Smith and Wesson in his left hand. The rag fell from the Mexican's hand, exposing a large caliber semi-automatic. Bill fired three times, striking him in the chest with all three shots.

Julie screamed as streams of blood flowed from the Mexican's back through the exit wounds caused by the .357. The pistol fell from his limp hand as a look of total surprise crossed his dying face.

Bill spun to face the phone booth, firing from his hip as the man inside tried to exit with a pistol in his hand. The first shot splintered the glass in the booth, blinding the would-be assassin. The second shot struck the telephone, tearing out a large chunk of the heavy black plastic. The last shot in his pistol struck the man in the temple, exploding the far side of his cranium, sending a mist of brains into the air.

Bill threw a twenty-dollar bill onto the attendant's body and jumped into the GTO. The engine roared to life and the rear tires lit up as the muscle car fishtailed from the gas pumps and onto the highway. Julie continued to scream.

"Shut her up!" shouted Bill above the roar of the engine.

Mike sat dazedly in the passenger seat, unmoving.

A mile out of town, Julie was no longer screaming. She hyperventilated, trying to catch her breath between half-sobs and half-screams. She kept shaking her head. Five minutes later, when she had not improved, Bill pulled the car to the side of the road and parked under a large cottonwood tree. He turned off the ignition and looked at Mike. "Do something with her."

Mike looked at him dumbly. "What the hell you want me to do? I'm not sure I can help myself, much less her."

"They were gonna kill us. What did you want me to do -- ask for forgiveness? I was committed to this when I shot those guys in that bar. Until we get to the States, when in doubt, I'm gonna shoot -- you got that?"

"Yeah, man, I got it. It seems pretty clear to me."

"Now, do something with her."

Julie whimpered and gasped for air alternately, her body convulsing with each gasp.

"I've never seen her like this, man. What the hell am I supposed to do?"

"You're a man, aren't you? Put your arm around her and tell her to relax or something. Hell, I don't know."

Julie looked at him for the first time since the shooting had started. The corners of her mouth turned down and she sobbed, "You really are going to take us back to jail, aren't you?"

"You just now discovered that?"

"I thought you might...change...your mind or something. But...you won't ...change...your mind. You're gonna take us...back to LA to rot...in jail for something...we didn't even do."

"That's up to the courts to decide, not me. I only get paid to bring you back, not try you." He looked over his shoulder. "Are you gonna be all right? We gotta get going."

"What the hell do you care? You go around killing people like most people shake hands. What the hell do you care about anything?" replied Julie.

"I care about living. And I care about getting you and Mike here back to LA." He pulled out a set of cuffs from behind his back. "C'mon, in the back seat with you. No more tourist."

When they were both cuffed, and his pistol reloaded, Bill resumed the trip east. Mike sat silently for several minutes, then said. "This is for real, isn't it?"

Bill glanced at him. "What is it with you two? You understand people going around trying to kill you, but you don't understand a regular guy trying to make a living?"

"A 'regular guy'? Is that what you said? If you're a 'regular guy', give me the crazies anytime. This is the late twentieth century, man. People don't go around bounty hunting for a living anymore," said Mike.

Bill shrugged. "Not many. The bails are generally too low for a man to make a decent living."

"My heart really bleeds for you, man."

"I didn't ask for it, so save your blood. You may need it."

The GTO purred down the highway at a steady 85 miles per hour. Bill looked in the rear-view mirror. Julie sat, staring at him. He smiled and winked at her. "Sure is a pretty day for a drive in the country, isn't it?"

She seemed to have recovered somewhat from the shooting scene. He saw the hint of a smile on her lips. "I should have met someone like you when I was in high school. Maybe my head would have been screwed on straight."

"A few minutes ago I was a creep."

"I've thought it over. You're right. If you had done anything else, we'd all be dead. How did you know the guy with the rag had a gun?"

"I didn't. But when he came out of the lube bay, he was wiping grease from his hands -- and his fingernails were clean. Yep, them fingernails will give you away every time."

She smiled broadly. "I guess you're not so dumb after all. Sorry I acted so stupid. It's just that I've never been that close to people being killed. It's bad enough to look at a dead body, but to see a person being blown apart is different." She paused. "How many people have you killed?"

"As a P I? Five I think -- assuming everyone I shot since I've been in Mexico is dead."

A sharp bend in the road took his attention from Julie as he put the car into a power slide.

"Hey, man, take it easy!" shouted Mike as the GTO wiggled a little before straightening out at the end of the curve.

A small canyon jutted off to their left, a narrow road running down its center, intersecting with Highway 2. "What's that?" asked Mike as the GTO sped by the canyon.

"That's the short way to the States -- through Naco. It's only about fifteen or so miles up the road."

"Why didn't you go that way?"

Bill thought of the last time he'd been in Naco and an involuntary shudder worked its way through his body. "That's not the safest way home. There's nothing in Naco but dopers and crooked cops, and most of them are looking for me. I'll pass. We'll be in Agua Prieta in an hour or so. Douglas is right across the line."

Suddenly Bill slowed the car.

"What's wrong?" asked Mike.

Bill nodded. "About half a mile up there on the right -- there's two cars parked under those trees."

"So?"

As they drew closer, Bill saw the board laying across the road. He couldn't see them at this distance, but he knew that board was full of nails. He slammed on the brakes and threw the transmission into reverse. The smell of burning rubber filled the air as the rear tires screamed against the rough asphalt. The GTO bounced and vibrated as it skipped backwards. Smoke obliterated their view of the two cars, only three hundred yards away.

The windshield shattered. The chattering sound of an automatic weapon followed. Bill spun the car around and headed in the opposite direction, bullets slamming into the Pontiac with sharp "thunks" as it rocked from side to side from the violent turn. In the rear-view mirror, Bill saw clouds of dust as the two cars spun onto the highway in pursuit.

"Is everybody all right?"

Mike brushed splintered glass from his hair and looked at Julie in the back seat. "We're alive if that's what you mean. We've had it, man. They've got machine guns."

"We're out of range. We can outrun 'em to Naco. It's not my first choice but the situation has changed a little."

"A little? A goddamned little? They're gonna kill us and make taco meat out of us and you say the situation has changed a little? Goddamn, man, take these cuffs off. We're trapped like rats if something happens to you. Please, man."

Bill fumbled in his pocket and withdrew a key. Still driving at more than ninety miles per hour on the two-lane road, he leaned over and unlocked one of Mike's cuffs. He handed him the key. "Take care of Julie. I've got some serious driving to do."

"You mean it gets worse?" Mike almost smiled.

The road to Naco was on them before Bill realized it was there. He put the GTO in a power-slide and roared north. Mike was thrown into him by the centrifugal force of the turn, nearly causing him to lose control of the car. When Mike was able to grab onto the seat and draw himself back to his knees, facing Julie, he glanced over at Bill. The two exchanged a quick glance. Bill shrugged.

Bill loved to drive fast, but he wished desperately the circumstances were different. He squinted his eyes against the wind blowing unobstructed through the shattered windshield. "Those guys did a number on my car."

"On your car? Your fucking car! Are you crazy? What about us?" shouted Mike.

Bill backhanded Mike. "We didn't get hit. My car did."

"Now why in the hell didn't I think of that?" Mike was making a visible effort not to retaliate.

Bill downshifted for a sharp curve. A pickup truck was parked across the road as he rounded the bend, two men in the back, automatic rifles pointed at them.

"Duck!" shouted Bill, just before the muzzle flashes erupted. "Shit!" The bullets thudded into the front of the car and what was left of the windshield. There was no room to get by the pickup without hitting a part of it. Bill chose the rear -- where the men were laying, firing their weapons. The right front fender of the GTO struck the pickup midway in the rear fender, slamming it forward and tipping it up on its side. As the right side of the big Pontiac rubbed the rear bumper of the pickup, the energy of the moving car toppled the other vehicle, crushing the men in the bed as it rolled over.

Bill became aware that Julie was screaming. Mike held his hands over his head to protect it from flying debris. Julie's torso hung over the back of the front seat. She struggled to push herself into the back and when she succeeded, she cut her bare legs on broken glass in the back seat. Her screams intensified.

Bill could smell burning rubber as the right front tire rubbed against the caved-in fender. It made a whining noise. He stopped the car and jumped out. "Mike! Help me pull this fender away from the tire! Quick!"

Mike jumped over the door and grabbed the fender. They grunted and strained and were able to move the fender away from the tire enough to allow straight driving without the tire rubbing. Turns would be different story. Bill saw a puddle of antifreeze growing under the radiator. Fear shot through him. "Get back in the car! They got the radiator. We gotta cover as much ground as we can while the old girl is still running."

They both jumped over the doors and into the seats. They took off in a cloud of dust and flying gravel.

"Jesus! Julie's cut. Her legs are bleeding," said Mike.

"Get in the back and stop the bleeding. When we get more distance between us and the bad guys, I've got a first aid kit in the trunk. Can't stop now. They gotta be close." Bill watched the temperature gauge begin to rise. The tire rubbed as he negotiated a turn. Julie whimpered in the back seat as Mike attended to her.

The road narrowed as they entered a small range of mountains. The smell of the rubbing tire mixed with the smell of hot metal as the engine temperature exceeded the capacity of the gauge. *Damn!* Bill knew the engine wouldn't run much longer. The valves started to clatter. *C'mon, baby. Just a little longer.*

A loud crash from the interior of the engine and it was all over. Steam and smoke billowed up through the cracks in the hood as Bill threw the transmission into neutral and coasted to a stop.

Mike sat in the back seat with Julie as Bill opened the trunk and withdrew a backpack. He handed the pack to Mike. "There's a first aid kit in there. Hurry. We've gotta get into those hills before our friends get here." He nodded to a small range of hills less than a mile north of where they sat.

The sounds of engines reached his ears as he bent over the trunk, picking up his survival gear. He turned and saw a Mercedes Benz and a late model Camaro racing around the curve behind them. Rifles hung out the windows of both vehicles. The ground around the GTO bubbled with little explosions as the bullets struck all around them, some of them chunking into the car.

"Oh, God! We're dead! Oh, sweet Jesus! What a way to go -- like a rat in a corner." Mike had stopped working on Julie's legs and sat unmoving.

"Patch her up, damnit!" Bill pulled out his Smith and took careful aim. At one hundred yards, he fired a shot. The windshield of the Mercedes shattered. Both cars turned and drove back up the road three or four hundred yards and parked well out of the accurate range of his pistol.

Bill turned to Mike. "Hurry up!"

Men spilled out of the two cars up the road. Bill counted five, though there could have been more. They spread out and opened fire again, their aim more accurate without the distraction of the moving vehicles to throw them off. Bill grabbed his canteen and Bowie knife from the trunk and moved to the front of the car in a low crouch. Mike and Julie were already there, hiding in front of the grille. Bill knelt next to them.

He noted the bandages on her legs. "How you doing?"

Bullets slammed into the car and the ground all around them.

"How am I doing? Fine. I'm just fine. Mike's got me all fixed up so I'll be in great shape when those bastards out there blow my brains out."

Bill looked around them. "I gotta admit, it doesn't look too good right now, but I'm not ready to roll over yet."

Mike nodded to the rear of the car. "You gonna take them on with those two pistols?" He ducked as a bullet whined within inches of his head. "Hell, all they gotta do is keep shooting. Eventually, they'll hit the gas tank just right and we'll all be a hole in the ground." He looked behind him. "And if we try for those rocks, our chances aren't too hot." He hesitated. "But they're better than staying here I guess."

Bill grabbed him by the arm. "You aren't going anyplace unless I tell you to. And I haven't told you to. So just sit tight."

"They're gonna kill us, man!" shouted Mike. "Can't you get that through your thick head? We're dead. Our best bet is to split up and run for it. At least one or two of us might make it."

Bill shook his head. "Bad plan, Mike. Real bad plan. If you go for it, I'll blow your brains out."

"What's the difference -- you or them?"

Bill grinned. "I'm a better shot -- and I'm a whole lot closer."

Their eyes locked for a moment as Mike thought it over. He looked at Julie.

"I believe him." she said. "The bastard would shoot us both."

Mike shrugged. "So, what's the plan? We just sit here and wait for them to blow us to hell or what?"

"If I can get to it, I have one more surprise for

them."

"What the hell can you possibly have than can help us outa this shit?"

Bill moved to the side of the car. "Be right back."

"Hey, man, where the hell are you going?"

Bill rushed for the open trunk and reached as far forward as he could. He removed a flap and pulled out the rifle, expecting at any second to feel the bite of a bullet in his body as slugs struck all around him, making dull plunking sounds when they hit the car. With the rifle and a bandoleer of ammunition in his hands, he rushed to the front of the car, falling down beside Julie as he rounded the front bumper. Her bandaged legs were only inches from his face as he looked up at her.

"Have I ever mentioned that you have two of the finest-looking legs I've ever seen -- even with bandages?" He glanced over at Mike. "No offense. It's simply a fact."

Despite their impossible situation, the ghost of a smile showed itself on Julie's lips. "You're a weird guy, Mister Bounty Hunter."

Bill rolled onto his stomach.

"What the hell is that?" asked Mike.

"M-1 Garand." Bill stuffed an eight-round clip into the receiver, pulled the bolt to the rear and released it. The rifle was ready to fire. He looked up at Mike. "What do you figure the distance to the nearest man?"

"Shit, I don't know -- what do I look like -- some kind of rangefinder? Maybe five or six hundred yards."

Bill nodded. "That's about what I figured." He ran the rear sight aperture up twenty-eight clicks, tested the wind with a wet finger and moved the crosswind knob two clicks right.

"You gonna try to shoot at this range without a scope?"

Bill nodded. "Used to do it all the time in the service. Course I was younger then." He smiled and moved closer to the front tire.

The men stood out in the open, confident they were invulnerable to return fire at that extreme range. Bill sighted down the barrel. His target looked no larger than a speck of pepper. Mike and Julie held their breaths as he drew a bead and waited. He took a breath, relaxed, aimed, took up the slack in the trigger and squeezed slowly. The rifle bucked into his shoulder. His target fell, almost in slow motion, seconds after the shot. As two men rushed to their fallen comrade's aid, Bill took careful aim and fired the remaining seven rounds rapid-fire. Both men went down, though he couldn't tell how badly either had been hit.

All firing stopped.

CHAPTER 8

Julie and Mike exhaled as one. Mike spoke first. "I don't believe that shit! I never saw anything like that in my life." He turned to Julie. "We got a chance of getting outa here. I mean, we really got a chance. This guy's a dead shot. Did you see them guys fall?"

Julie smiled. "Now what, Mister Bounty Hunter? Is this what they had in mind when they came up with the term 'Mexican stand off'? I always wondered how those things got resolved, or if they just stood each other off until they all starved to death."

Bill put another clip into the M-1. "Don't know. Never been involved in one. I suggest we get our gear ready to make a dash for those hills. I'm going to crawl to the back of the car and poke a hole in the gas tank -- get rid of the explosive potential if I can cover the gas with sand and split the tank with my knife. If we do that, we can hold out until dark -- and once it's dark we can hoof it into Naco."

"Unless he's got more hoods waiting for us between here and there," said Julie.

"Whoever 'he' is probably does. Looks to me like you guys aggravated somebody with a lot of money and power."

"That's what we been trying to tell you. Now do

you believe us?" said Mike.

"I know they're mad at you, but I don't know if it's because you killed one of them or if you ripped them off like you said." Bill shrugged. "It doesn't really matter. You're going back to the States for trial."

Mike thumped his knee with a closed fist. "What the hell's the matter with you? We didn't do anything but steal dope money from dealers. We can all get out of this together -- and rich." He looked at Julie, then back to Bill. "We'll share it equally -- three way split."

"That's real magnanimous of you, Mike, old buddy -- but I'm not interested."

Julie gave Mike a look, threw her hands up, palms upward, and shrugged. "I don't know what's wrong with him."

"I told you, I don't deal with bounties and blackmailers."

"Jesus Christ, here we go again. Get off your soapbox for a minute, man," said Mike.

"Forget it, Mike. Let him be. If he wants to die broke, let him."

Bill shot her a quick glance. "I don't care how much money I've got when I die, it's how much I've got while I'm alive that concerns me." He smiled.

"I swear, you're a weirdo, Mister Bounty Hunter."

"How are your legs?"

"Lousy, you want to give them a closer inspection? Is that what you want?"

Bill stared at her. "I've almost had enough of you, you know that?"

"You haven't had any of me, Mister Bounty Hunter, and if you ever do, I'll be dead."

"Shut up and sit back against the grille of the car."

"A little kinky, huh?"

"Just do it." He looked at Mike. "Did you put some of the bacitracin ointment on those cuts?"

"Baci. . .what?"

"Never mind." He knelt next to Julie and unceremoniously ripped off one of the three bandages on her left leg.

"Ow! Goddamn! What is this, some new kind of Chinese torture?"

"Be quiet." He studied the laceration. It was irregular, about two inches long, but it wasn't deep. He pulled a tube of bacitracin ointment from his first aid kit and squeezed some of it into the wound, then placed a fresh bandage on it and repeated the process with her other wounds. She bit her lip, but made no sounds as he unfeelingly tore each of the old bandages off.

Her skin was soft and silky to his touch, and he wanted done with the job before he thought about changing his policy regarding bounties. When he finished, he looked up at her face. She was smiling.

"You find something funny?" he asked.

"You. Except for the macho way you pulled the tape off, you've got the most gentle touch I ever felt." She reached out and brushed her fingers through his hair.

Bill backed away. "That won't work, lady. Nice try though."

A single bullet smashed into the fender near where he knelt. The thump of the impacting bullet was followed by the report of the rifle. They all lay flat on the ground.

Bill picked up his M-1, lying next to Julie's foot. "They've got a scoped rifle out there."

A treble voice blared over a loudspeaker. "You down there by the car. We wish to talk to you. We will meet you halfway under a white flag."

Bill smiled at Mike. "Not with that scoped rifle out there, they won't." He leaned around the tire and fired three quick shots in the direction of the loudspeaker.

The sound of the speaker being dropped was amplified to their position. A moment later the voice said. "I see you are not such a dumb gringo. I tell you what. We let you go if you give us those two with you."

Bill fired another shot in the general direction of the sound.

After a short pause, the speaker resumed. "You are a very difficult man to deal with, *señor*. Very well, I am authorized to offer you one hundred thousand dollars in cash to give them back to us. What do you say to that?"

Bill fired another round.

"That's it, Mister Bounty Hunter. You stick to your guns. Remember, you don't deal with bounties or blackmailers," snorted Julie.

The speaker blared again. "I have one final offer for you, mister gringo. It is a good one. I will give you two hundred thousand dollars in cash and let you have one hour alone with the woman before we take her. Now, how can you refuse such a generous offer?"

Bill looked Julie up and down. "You know, that *is* a mighty tempting offer."

"You sonofabitch!"

Bill smiled. He fired three shots and reloaded quickly when the spent clip ejected from the receiver with a resounding ping. When he looked up at Julie, she was smiling again.

"Were you tempted -- just a little bit?" she asked, her smile widening.

"I'll never tell the truth on that one, so don't ask me again."

A bullet slammed into the front tire, deflating it instantly. They hugged the ground. "Damn! That tire only had about four thousand miles on it," said Bill.

"I'll buy you a new tire if we get out of this," said Mike.

"You bet your bippy you will," said Bill, his face still in the dirt.

"So, what's the plan?" asked Mike.

"There can't be more than two or three of them left. After dark, I figure on takin' 'em out and stealing one of their cars. It's still a long walk to the border."

Julie tapped him on the shoulder. "Excuse me? Does 'taking them out' mean you're going to go up there after them and try to kill them by yourself?"

"Unless you want to come along."

"No thanks."

Bill turned his head. "How about you, Mike, you in to a little guerrilla warfare?"

"You're crazy, man."

Bill nodded. "Yeah, I know." He raised his head and looked up the canyon. "We're gonna have to be sure they don't flank us. Mike, you watch the canyon on the right; I'll watch the left; Julie, you watch the north, behind us, in case one of 'em gets by Mike or me."

Mike said nothing, but moved to his assigned spot.

Julie said, "You're the general -- for now."

The day wore on. Occasionally, the man with the

rifle took a shot, and though he was always close, he never scored a hit on any of them. It was almost dark when the other cars arrived. Bill's heart sank when he saw the first car stop in a cloud of dust behind the others, but with the arrival of three more, he almost gave up hope.

"Mike, pick up the backpack and get ready to run for those rocks north of us. We can't wait any longer for them to get out of those cars and get into position. Julie, grab what you can carry and follow Mike when I say go. You got it?"

"What are you going to do?" she asked.

"I'm going to give you cover until you hit the rocks. Now get ready."

She scooped up the canteen and knelt next to him. "How are you going to get to the rocks?" she whispered.

"On my feet -- just as fast as they'll carry me." He turned to Mike. "You ready?"

Mike nodded.

"Go!" Bill fired an eight-round clip, spreading his bullets in a fan. When the empty clip ejected from the receiver, he jammed in another and fired eight more. He was on his third clip when sporadic fire came from the area of the parked cars. The firing intensified until the little canyon echoed with the reports of the automatic weapons. The GTO sank to the ground as the remaining three tires were struck by random slugs. Dust filled the air around him, smothering the oxygen, causing Bill to gasp for breath.

An overzealous Mexican drove one of the cars down the road at the GTO. Bill emptied a clip into the windshield as it approached. The windshield shattered and the car, a late model Ford, careened into the canyon wall on Bill's left. The flying lead drove him back to the ground while he reloaded and cursed himself for not waiting a bit longer to fire at the Ford. He might have been able to capture it.

He looked behind him. Mike and Julie were nowhere to be seen. With one last look at the group of cars up the road, he fired two rounds and dashed madly for the rocks behind him, his heart beating wildly in his head, his throat constricted with fear. He jumped into a small wash and out the other side, fear giving him the speed of a gazelle and the strength of an elephant. He was only twenty yards from the rocks when he saw Julie laying on the ground behind a small mound of dirt. He fell prone and slid to a stop next to her, his arms raw and bleeding from the slide.

Julie's arms were wrapped over her head, the canteen lying on the ground at her side. "Julie! Are you hit?" He rolled her onto her back.

"Ow!" she moaned.

"What is it? I don't see any blood."

"My ankle. I twisted my ankle."

Bill looked over his shoulder. A small army of fifteen or twenty men made its way cautiously down the canyon, some of the men fired their weapons at the GTO, others in the general direction of the rocks, only twenty yards from where Bill and Julie lay.

"C'mon, Julie, you've gotta get up and run."

"I can't! I can't! It hurts damnit!" Tears ran down her cheeks.

Bill slung the M-1 and canteen over his shoulder and picked her up in his arms. He stumbled and ran the last twenty yards to the cover of the rocks, banging his knee and tearing his trouser leg as he stepped behind cover. He clenched his teeth and managed not to fall with Julie, but his knee hurt as he laid her gently on the ground.

He stepped back to the rocks facing up the canyon and un-slung his rifle. He took careful aim and fired, dropping one of the advancing Mexicans. The others stopped and hunted cover. Bill leaned the M-1 against a large boulder and turned to Mike, who knelt next to him, cowering against his cover. Without warning, Bill punched him in the face, sending Mike reeling backwards.

Mike got back to his knees and spit blood from his mouth. "What the hell was that for?"

"You sorry sonofabitch! What the hell were you gonna do -- leave her out there to get killed?" Bill pulled out his Bowie knife. "I oughta kill you right now and save myself a lot of trouble."

Mike held his hands up, palms out. "I swear to God, man, I didn't know she was out there. I thought she made it with me. Hell, I was huggin' that rock and had my eyes shut tight as hell. I swear, man, I didn't even know."

"You're a damned liar!"

"I swear to you, man. She's all the family I have left. I'd risk my life for her in a minute. I swear it."

Bill lowered his knife. "She's what?"

"I'm his sister, Mister Bounty Hunter -- not his live-in -- like everybody thinks."

Bill sheathed his knife and looked them both over. "You two are full of surprises, aren't you? I wonder what it is with people lately. Nobody wants anybody to know they're related." He looked at the darkening sky, dismissing the thoughts running through his mind. "It'll be dark in a few more minutes, then we cut through the hills. They'll probably stay on or near the road, so we ought to have it pretty easy going from here to Naco."

"I can't walk. I'm telling you, my ankle is killing me," said Julie.

Bill knelt next to her. "Mike, watch the canyon while I try to do something with Julie's ankle."

"You got it, man." Mike moved into a position to watch the road running through the canyon.

"Why don't you kiss it and make it better?" cooed Julie.

Bill looked at the ankle. "It's too ugly to kiss. It's already about twice the size it should be."

She pouted while he pulled an elastic bandage from the first aid kit. He wrapped the ankle as tightly as he could without cutting off her circulation, despite her numerous protests of pain. When he completed the task, he held the bandaged ankle gently in his hands and looked into her eyes in the waning light.

"It wasn't really too ugly to kiss." He stood and moved to the rocks, near Mike, embarrassed by what he had said. He didn't know why he had said it.

Suddenly there was a blinding flash on the road below, and the GTO was gone, along with four or five Mexicans who stood near the car when it exploded. Mike ducked behind the rocks. "Jesus Christ! What the hell was that?"

Bill clucked. "A fitting end to a fine car. More precisely, about thirty pounds of C-4 plastic explosive."

"Plastic explosive? What the hell are you -- some kind of nut?"

"Maybe -- but it cut the odds down a little bit -- by four or five, I'd say."

Julie looked at him questioningly.

Bill shrugged. "I couldn't stand the thought of a bunch of creeps getting their hands on my car."

"What set it off?" asked Mike.

Bill pulled a small key from his pocket and threw it into the rocks. "Me and Westclock. I armed it just before you guys made your dash." He looked at the gathering crowd in the darkness of the canyon. "Pretty good timing too, if I do say so."

"Jesus, remind me never to mess with one of your cars," said Mike.

"You won't have a chance to if we don't get out of here. We'll take turns carrying Julie. I'll carry all the gear for a while and you pack Julie as long as you can."

"Hey, that ain't right."

"You're the prisoner, Mike. Don't push your luck, or you'll be carrying her all the way to Naco."

Mike said something under his breath and looked at his sister. "C'mon, damnit. Piggy back, just like we used to play when we were kids."

Julie smiled. "Oh boy, this is fun." She looked at Bill. "Can we play this some more, daddy?"

"Let's get moving."

Julie's lighthearted mood changed rapidly once on the move. It soon became apparent that traversing the hills without the benefit of trails was a more difficult task than Mike was up to with her on his back. In less than twenty minutes, he collapsed to the ground. Julie narrowly missed injuring her other ankle in the fall.

Bill turned from his point position and knelt in the

darkness. "Is everybody all right?"

Mike gasped for breath. "You know, I'm...getting tired of...you...asking us that. Everything was fine...until you came...into my life. I was all right then."

Bill ignored him. "How about you, Julie -- how's the ankle?"

Her voice was soft. "I don't think you guys can make it if you have to carry me. It's too much."

"I can make it, sis. Just give me a minute to catch my breath."

"No time for that," said Bill. He slung his rifle and placed the canteen and backpack on the ground. "Grab the gear and let's get moving. I've got Julie."

Without another word, he helped Julie to her feet. Once she was in position on his back, he stepped out in the darkness, Mike behind him. He said nothing to Julie, who rode comfortably on his back. Her firm legs felt good against the inside of his elbows as he trudged the uneven terrain. He forced his mind to think of other things.

He wondered what Laura was doing. He wondered if it would do him any good to think about her. She was certainly a beautiful woman -- a classic beauty -- not like Julie. Julie was "Hollywood" beautiful. Beautiful, and sexy. Damn! He was back to Julie.

"Ow!" Her foot brushed against a bush as he walked by it in the darkness.

"Sorry."

"That's okay."

He waited for more, but that was all she said. She must be getting tired. Speaking of tired, he was beginning to feel the weight now. How long had he been carrying her -- twenty minutes -- an hour? He stiffened his jaw and hiked her up higher on his back as gently as possible.

"Getting tired, Bounty Hunter?"

"What happened to 'Mister Bounty Hunter'?"

"Since we've been so close this last hour or two, I thought I'd drop the formalities if it's all right with you."

Bill nodded, "That's fine."

"I think you better rest."

"I can go a little bit longer."

"I've got to go to the bathroom."

Bill stopped. Mike nearly walked into him. "What's going on? You need a break? I can't believe you carried her this long."

"She's gotta go to the bathroom. There's some tissue paper in the first aid kit. Hand it to me. I'll take her off to those rocks on the right."

Mike complied quickly, eager to get the pack from his weary and chafing shoulders. Bill carried Julie to the rocks and sat her down gently. When he turned to leave, she said. "Don't go too far, okay?"

Bill nodded, a gesture wasted in the darkness. "I'll only be about fifteen or so yards away."

"Okay."

He walked stiffly back to Mike who lay on his back, his head resting on the first aid kit. "You're gonna have to carry her for awhile. I'm about give out."

"You ought to be. Christ, you been carryin' her for almost two hours. How the hell do you do it?"

"It's almost a pleasure, Mike, old man, but I'm afraid I've had about as much pleasure as I can stand for a while."

"Why don't we rest for a while? It can't be that much further to Naco, can it?"

"No, I don't think so, but we still have to steal a car and get across the line."

"We're gonna steal a car?"

"Yeah, and it's gotta have American plates."

"Kinda picky, aren't you?"

"It makes things a whole lot easier if we don't have to run the port. We'll just come back as tourists."

"Makes sense to me. The only trouble is, I'm not all that crazy about going back."

"You wanna stay down here with your Mexican friends?"

"I'll pass on that."

"Hey, what's taking Julie so long?"

Mike giggled. "You sure been showing a lot of interest in her since you found out she was my sister."

"Stow it, Mike." His tone was serious. "I'm gonna see what's taking her so long. You sit tight."

He walked cautiously back to where he had left Julie. When he was only a few feet from where he had last seen her, he whispered, "Julie, you there?"

"Where have you been?" There was concern in her whispered voice.

"Where have I been? I've been waiting for you to call me." She was barely visible in the late, half-moon light.

"I did, but you didn't answer."

"You should have called a little louder."

There was a short silence. "I was afraid, Bounty Hunter. There, are you happy?"

"No, Julie, I'm not happy, okay? I'm not happy about any of this. Now, are *you* happy?"

"But you're gonna take us back anyway, right?"

"Afraid so. C'mon, hop on. I'll get you back to Mike."

They rested for thirty minutes, during which time Bill smoked two cigarettes, cupping each one to hid the embers. He sipped lightly of the water and stood painstakingly. "I guess we better get going. That moon will help us, but it helps them too, so we'd better be a little more careful. Can you handle Julie for a while, Mike?"

"Yeah, but not as long as you did, man, so keep that in mind."

"Okay, let's go."

The pack, rifle and canteen seemed even heavier than Julie had been. He knew he was reaching his physical limit. He shouldn't have carried her so long without resting. He knew better. He remembered *Operation Prairie II* in Vietnam. He had carried too much weight then -- for all of those who could go no further with what they had -- he carried their loads as well as his own. If nightfall hadn't stopped the battalion's advance, he wouldn't have made it -- or would he?

"Hey, man." Mike's voice broke into his reverie. He stopped and turned around.

"I can't go any farther, man," Mike panted. He let Julie gently to the ground. She hobbled to a mesquite tree and leaned against it.

"Here, take this stuff. I'll take her."

Julie weighed a ton. He knew she was much closer to a hundred and twenty pounds than she was a ton, but his mind wasn't convinced. In less than an hour, he stopped, his legs shaking and his blood pulsing in his temples.

"Break," he panted.

Mike dropped the canteen and pack to the ground. He fell unceremoniously in a heap on top of the pile. Bill let Julie down gently, nearly losing his balance in the process.

"You've about had it, haven't you, Bounty Hunter?" said Julie.

"I'll make it, don't you worry yourself about me. I just think now's as good a time as any to take a break."

"Sure." She sat on the rough ground.

Bill sat between her and Mike. He lay on his back and rested his head in his hands. Julie lay her head on his stomach. He jumped with a start.

"Relax, Bounty Hunter. I could use a pillow, if you don't mind."

He relaxed and closed his eyes as she nestled the back of her head into his aching stomach.

"Umm. That feels good, Bounty Hunter. Thanks."

Mike snored peacefully at their side.

"My pleasure."

"Hey, Bounty Hunter?"

"Yeah?" He was half-asleep.

"You got a wife or steady girl?"

"No wife. Had one once."

"What happened?"

"Didn't work out."

"How about a steady girl?"

"You interested?"

"I might be."

"Forget it. I'm takin' you and Mike in."

"I know, Bounty Hunter. You said that once before."

"You mean after you serve your twenty-to-life for

murder, you might want to be my girl? I'm afraid I'm too old to wait that long. I'm almost old enough to be your father. I *am* old enough to be your father."

"You're not my father."

"Get some rest."

"You think I'm kidding."

"I think you better be. My reputation in this business is impeccable. I intend to keep it that way. Get some rest."

"I'm sorry I twisted my ankle."

"So am I."

CHAPTER 9

Bill awakened to the smell of Julie's hair. She was snuggled up to him, her face buried in his neck. With his left hand, he reached around her face and brushed the hair from her eyes. She moved closer into him. He let his arm fall around her shoulders and hold her gently. His mind began to drift to Laura.

"It would be worth the wait."

Her sleepy voice startled him. He pulled his arm from her shoulders and lay it on the ground. She put both of her arms around him and held him tightly, snuggling her nose into the curve of his neck under his chin. "It's cold, Bounty Hunter. That's all. It's just cold."

"I'll take my shirt off and cover your legs."

"I'm cold around my shoulders. Put your arm around me. It felt good."

Nervously, like an inexperienced high school freshman, he tentatively put his arm around her shoulders.

"Tighter please. It's cold out here."

He held her firmly and felt her body pressed against his. She was right, it did feel good.

"Your reputation is safe with me, Bounty Hunter." After a moment of silence, she said, "Life is sure screwed up sometimes, you know that?"

"Get some rest."

"I don't want any rest. I want to enjoy this as long as I can. You know what?"

"No. What?"

"I feel better right now than I ever have with any man. That's crazy, isn't it?"

"Julie, it won't work. I'm taking you in."

"Shut up, damn you. Don't say that anymore." She moved up his body until her cheek rested against his. He felt the warmth of her tears against his face. "Just don't say anything else."

He kissed her salty cheek and fell asleep, his arms wrapped around her.

"Get up, you sonofabitch!"

Bill opened his eyes. Julie was still on top of him. He felt her eyelashes flutter against his cheek. "Mike, what are you doing?" she said sleepily.

"This sonofabitch thinks he can do what he wants with you, just because he's got the guns. Well, I've got the big gun now, you bastard. Get away from my sister."

"Take it easy, Mike. This isn't what you think," said Bill.

"What do I think, you horny bastard? Get off him, Julie. I'm gonna blow his brains out."

"Mike, damn it, leave him alone. He didn't do anything." She remained on top of him.

"Bullshit. Get offa him, I'm gonna blow his fucking brains out."

"Mike, I told you about your language," said Bill.

"Are you crazy or what? I'm about to blow your brains out, and you're giving me a lecture on etiquette?"

"Sit up, Julie," said Bill.

She didn't move. "Mike, so help me -- put that gun down."

Bill pulled his Walther out from behind his back and pointed it at Mike. "Lay it down real gentle, Mike. Julie, get up."

"You may get me, bad-ass, but you're dead."

Bill clucked. "Mike, Mike, Mike. I've got all the ammo. You don't think I'd give you a loaded rifle, do you? You might shoot it and bring down half of the bad guys in the world on us."

Mike looked at him, then to Julie, then to the rifle. Bill cocked the hammer on the Walther. Mike turned and placed the rifle carefully on the backpack. "You sonofabitch."

Bill stood and walked stiffly to the M-1. He uncocked the Walther and put in the inside waistband holster at his back and picked up the rifle. "Remind me never to trust my better judgement again." He pulled the bolt to the rear, ejecting a live round. He picked up the round and put it in his pocket. He ejected the clip and put it in the bandoleer strap and handed Mike the rifle. "Take care of it. It's the best weapon we've got."

"I could have pulled the trigger, thinking I had an empty rifle."

"That thought occurred to me after I said it, but I had to play it out." Bill's legs felt like rubber. He looked up at the moon. "We slept too long. We've gotta get going. Julie, you ready?"

She climbed onto his back and they continued north. Ten minutes into their journey, Julie said, "How have you lived so long?"

"You been wondering about that all this time?"

"The thought has occurred to me several times since we started walking. Is that what happened to your marriage -- she got tired of waiting for you to get killed?"

"That was part of it."

He felt her nod. "I can believe that. You know, if I live long enough, you're going to have to find a steady job. I don't want you doing this kind of stuff anymore."

Bill laughed softly. "I'm beginning to like your sense of humor. It took me a while to get used to it, but I think I like it."

"Who's kidding?"

She rode easily on his back, her breasts pressed against him, her arms around his neck. The town of Naco appeared in the distance as they rounded a small hill, the lights standing in stark contrast to the darkness of the desert.

Bill put Julie on a small boulder and handed Mike the bandoleer of ammunition for the M-1. "You know how to load it?"

"I'll figure it out."

"Give it to me."

Bill gave Mike a quick lesson and handed the rifle back to him. "I'll be back as soon as I can find a car."

"What happens if you don't find one?" asked Mike.

"I left you the rifle, what more do you want?"

"I want you to come back with a car."

"I'll do my best."

"How do we know you won't just walk across the border and forget about us?"

Bill raised an eyebrow. "After what they did to my car? Get serious, Mike. Besides, if I was gonna do that, I sure wouldn't leave that rifle with you. I'll be back."

"They're in town, you know," said Julie.

Bill turned to Julie. "Yeah, I imagine. Can't do much about that except try to stay out of their way."

"Is that money worth all of this to you?" she asked.

"To tell you the truth, I didn't have it pictured like this. But once I shot those guys in Guaymas, I was committed. I'd be running now, with or without you two. I might as well get something for it, don't you think?"

"Hell no," said Mike.

"Thanks, pal." He turned and walked toward town.

"Good luck, Bounty Hunter," said Julie as he walked the gentle slope into town. He waved at her over his shoulder, not looking back.

The sky was just beginning to turn grey in the east as he walked into town from the southwest. He knew where he was going to search for that car with American plates.

Frederico Gonzales had eluded him on his last trip down here, but Bill knew where to find him. He had almost been killed getting the information to the Pima County Sheriff's Department. He had managed to escape by crossing the border on foot two miles west of the port of entry and walking back to the port for his car.

Two blocks south of the fence marking the international border, and three blocks west of the port of entry, sat the 1970 Hemi Challenger belonging to Gonzales. The plates were expired, but that made little difference here -- Gonzales paid his dues to the local police on a regular basis. Without the expired Arizona plate, Bill would have been able to pick this car out in a crowd of a thousand. The bright orange paint job was oxidizing from lack of care, but the car still stood out.

Bill approached the car cautiously. It was parked halfway onto the sidewalk in front of the apartment Gonzales used as a crash house. He knew there would be at least two or three others in the house with Gonzales -- it seems like drug dealers can't do without a crowd around them. The friends had Uzi sub-machine guns the last time he had seen them. Bill smiled as he thought of the one-sided odds the last time he had come down here. He felt the Walther at his back and the Smith on his hip. *Not much has changed.*

Now that he was this close, it was a matter of pride. They were probably sleeping one off. He tried the front door. It was unlocked. *Talk about confidence!* He opened it and stepped inside.

The small front room of the house smelled of incense and old urine. Two Uzis stood, barrels up, against the love seat. He picked one of them up and quietly checked the magazine. It was loaded. There were two small bedrooms in the rear of the house. In the first one, two men and three women lay on a large mattress, placed carelessly on the floor, naked from head to toe and out cold. Bill moved stealthily to the next room.

Gonzales lay atop a sheet, dressed only in his shorts. A young woman lay with him, her face in his lap. Bill tiptoed into the room and put the barrel of the Uzi under Gonzales's chin. "Good morning, glory. Rise and shine."

Gonzales opened his eyes sluggishly. The young woman sat up. Bill put his finger to his lips. She sat silently. He looked down at Gonzales. "Mornin', Freddy. You've never met me face-to-face before. The name's Bill

Rutledge, Private Investigator. Grab your pants and shoes. We're gonna visit a judge in Pima County."

"You're fuckin' crazy, man."

Bill jammed the barrel up under Gonzales's chin so hard, he thought it was going to exit under the man's tongue. "Now, Freddy. One wrong move -- one sound -- and I blow your brains all over the ceiling. You understand?"

Gonzales nodded, moving the barrel of the Uzi up and down as his head bobbed back and forth. Bill pulled the Uzi out of his throat and said to the girl. "You -- get some clothes on." He motioned for her to dress. Quickly she responded, slipping a cotton dress over her head.

When Gonzales was dressed, Bill grabbed his arms and cuffed his hands behind him. "The keys to your car, Freddy -- where are they?"

"On the dresser, man. You're a dead man, you know that."

"Shut up, Freddy, or you won't be around to see that happen." He picked up the keys on the top of the dresser. "Let's go. Quietly."

He picked up the other Uzi on the way out the door. He put the girl in the back seat, Freddy up front with him. The car started instantly, the high-powered hemi rocking the chassis as it idled. Bill put it in low gear and drove away from the apartment, a feeling of elation washing through his body. *I did it! I got the untouchable Frederico Gonzales.* He felt more accomplishment with Gonzales than he did with Mike and Julie. Too bad Pima County only offered a four-thousand-dollar reward. No wonder he was untouchable -- he wasn't worth the risk.

He drove past two men standing by a pickup truck

on the south side of town, the sub-machineguns in the bed plainly visible as they passed. He smiled and waved at them.

"Hey, man, where the hell are you going? This isn't the way to the States," said Frederico.

"Oh, I forgot to tell you, we've got to pick up a couple of friends of mine first."

"Are you crazy, man? You think this is some kind of funny game or something? My guys will have your balls on the hood of this car in an hour."

"Freddy, you should watch your language in front of a lady." He smiled and nodded at the woman in the back seat.

"You mean my whore? She can't understand English, man. All she's good for is a piece of ass, and she isn't even much good for that."

Bill reached out and backhanded Frederico across the mouth. "Shut up, Freddy. I don't want to hear anymore garbage from you. I'm tired of listening to people who don't give a damn about other people's feelings. Open it again, and I'll give you a tonsillectomy with a .357 magnum and take your empty head back for my bounty."

Frederico glared at him silently. Bill watched the woman in the back seat carefully in the mirror. He turned off the road and drove across the sagebrush and through small washes, the Challenger bottoming out several times.

"Hey, man, you're fucking up my car!"

"Shut up, Freddy. I don't want to hear it. This thing will be a bucket of rust before you get out. Don't worry about it." He stopped the car short of a small ravine and stepped out onto the desert soil. Mike came running down the small wash, Julie hobbling behind him, their faces beaming.

"You did it! You did it! It's even got Americ..." Julie noticed the two passengers. "Who are they?"

"Long story." When Mike was in range, he grabbed the rifle from him and cuffed his hands.

"Oh no, not this shit again. I thought we were coming to some sort of understanding."

"Not yet, Mike. Not yet." He motioned to the woman in the back seat. "Freddy, tell her to get out. Apologize for me, but she's gonna have to walk back to town." He looked at Mike and Julie. "By the time she gets there, we'll be long gone."

"Who are they?" repeated Julie.

"I don't know who the woman is, but Freddy here is a bad boy. He's wanted in Arizona for three counts of armed robbery, three counts of kidnapping, four counts of assault with intent to commit murder and two counts of escape." He dropped his head to the window. "Did I forget anything, Freddy?"

"Yeah, man -- murder. I'm gonna kill your ass and put your head on a pole in Naco for everyone to see."

Bill winked at him. "How long you been having these delusions, Freddy?"

Frederico mumbled something unintelligible while the woman got out of the car and started her long walk back to town.

"Mike, you and Julie in the back. Mike, you lay low until I give you the word. There's a pickup on the road between here and town with a couple of our friends waiting for us. They got a good look at me and Freddy and the woman coming out here. I'm hoping they'll think it's the same three coming back."

Julie stood silently looking at him as Mike entered the car awkwardly with his hands cuffed behind his back. "Why did you bring him? Isn't two hundred thousand dollars enough for you? How much is he worth, a million?"

"Four thousand dollars."

"Four thousand dollars? Four thousand dollars? I wouldn't think him hardly worth your effort."

"It's a real long story, Julie. C'mon, get in the car. I'll help you." He reached for her arm.

She jerked away at his touch. "Leave me alone. I'll manage without your help." She hobbled to the door, folded the driver's seat forward and sat back heavily in the rear seat.

"Caramba! I see what you do with your time, gringo. I'll bet she was a good lay, no?"

Bill was halfway into the driver's seat when Frederico made his remark. He jumped out of the car and walked to the passenger door, opening it deliberately, almost able to control his rage, but the calmness left him when he opened the door and saw the smirk on Frederico's face.

He grabbed Frederico by the shoulders and pulled him from the car, shoving him face first into the dirt. He jumped on Frederico's back and roughly uncuffed his prisoner, then jerked him to his feet. With as much power as he had in his body, he hit Frederico in the face. The little Mexican went down like a wet sack of potatoes. Bill stood near him, his legs spread, breathing heavily. "Get up, you little slime ball."

Frederico rolled onto his stomach, tried to regain his feet, and stumbled back to the ground. He propped himself up on one elbow. "You're a big man, gringo when the odds are in your favor."

"Isn't that the way you play, Freddy, you little sonofabitch?"

Frederico remained motionless.

Bill tossed his Walther to the ground in front of the fallen man.

"No! What are you doing?" screamed Julie.

"Hey, man, are you crazy?" shouted Mike.

Julie opened the door of the car and fell in her haste to exit. She braced herself on the side of the car and followed its outline until she was on the passenger side, only a few feet away from Bill and Frederico.

"Go ahead, Freddy. Pick it up. I want this more than I wanted to talk to Santa Claus when I was a kid. Go ahead." His hand was positioned above the holster on his left hip, the Smith and Wesson hanging there menacingly.

Frederico smiled, his teeth solid red from the blood running out his nose, gums and torn lips. "You *are* crazy, gringo. But I don't think I'll try it. You won't shoot me if I don't -- not in front of two witnesses."

"Don't count on it, you bastard." All of the years of frustration with the court system and the injustice of the justice system flowed into his consciousness. Though his remark about Julie had been the catalyst for his anger, she was forgotten, his anger replaced by the hopelessness of it all. He pulled the Smith from the holster and pointed it at Frederico's head.

Frederico's expression turned to raw fear. His eyes darted to the small hills behind him, then to the

Walther laying in the dirt. They came to rest on Bill's drawn face, eyes narrowed, mouth set.

Bill saw the fear in Frederico's eyes and reveled in it as his finger took up the slack in the trigger. "So long, Freddy."

"No!" Julie's ear-piercing scream echoed into the hills as she fell forward, grabbing him around the torso and holding on for dear life.

Bill loosed his hold on the trigger and kept an eye on Frederico and the Walther while he tried to push her away.

"No! Please! Please! No!" She was crying, sobbing.

Bill felt his knees trembling.

Mike shouted from the back seat of the Challenger. "Goddamn, man, get a grip. What the hell's happened to you? Shit!"

"You won't be any better than he is if you kill him, Bounty Hunter," sobbed Julie.

Bill looked down at her tear-streaked face as she held tightly to him. "I don't know that I am." He bent down and picked the Walther from the ground, Julie still clinging to him. Relief spread across Frederico's face. Bill holstered the Smith and tucked the Walther into the holster at the small of his back.

"I'll help you to the car," he said quietly.

Julie sobbed on his arm as they made their way around the car. He helped her inside and averted Mike's look of surprise as he pulled the seat back and went back for Frederico, who remained in position. He cuffed his prisoner carefully and deliberately and escorted him to the passenger seat.

He started the car and put it into gear. No one spoke as they approached the pickup on the road. Mike put his head down and they drove peacefully by the roadblock, Bill waving silently, a phony smile plastered on his face. Still no one spoke.

Frederico was the first to break the silence as they drove into the awakening town. "Looks like you lose, cowboy."

Bill stopped the car four blocks south of the port and stared at the group of men milling around the small guardhouse on the outbound Mexican side of the border.

"Jesus, there must be twenty of 'em," said Mike from the back seat.

Frederico smirked. "You give me the weapons and I'll let you keep the woman and go."

Bill said nothing. He shut the engine off and stepped back to the trunk. He opened it and withdrew the Uzis and the M-1, then walked back to the driver's seat and sat behind the wheel.

"That's better, cowboy. We let bygones be bygones, okay?"

Bill could see the fear on the faces of Mike and Julie in the back seat in the rear-view mirror. Silently, he cocked each Uzi and took the safety off the M-1. He placed the M-1 along his left side, between him and the door. The Uzis, he lay on his lap, barrels pointing outward. He pulled the Walther from behind his back and jacked a round into the chamber. He released the hammer slowly and re-holstered. Calmly, he checked the cylinder of the Smith and re-holstered.

"It's a bluff, cowboy. You aren't that crazy."

Slowly and deliberately, he started the engine and

put the transmission into first gear. He turned his head and said, "I'm sorry for both of you. This part wasn't your fight."

"You aren't going to try to bust the gate with all those guns there, are you?" asked Mike.

"We have no choice. We're too close." Bill saw a small crowd gathering on the American side of the line, mostly Immigration and Naturalization people, but he thought he saw at least one Border Patrol in the group. They knew something was up.

"Hey, cowboy, think it over, man. Let me talk to my people. Keep the guns. Let me go and we'll let all across. Hell, man, you can even take my car, man."

"I don't make deals with bounties." He leaned out the window, one of the Uzis in his hand, released the clutch and mashed the accelerator pedal to the floor.

CHAPTER 10

The roar of the 426 cubic inch hemi engine drowned out Julie's screams as they sped for the international border. People on the sidewalks ducked for cover as the men at the gate opened up with a wall of automatic weapons. Bill squeezed the trigger on his Uzi and felt it buck in his hand, almost falling free of his grasp. He released the trigger, got a firmer grip, and squeezed again, holding the trigger down until the magazine was empty.

The line of men covering their escape exploded in all directions as each man lost his nerve and sought shelter. The windshield on the Challenger disintegrated, sending glass flying into the interior of the car. Bill felt something punch into his upper chest, near his right shoulder. It slammed him against the seat. He felt the impact of heavy slugs as they ripped into the interior and sheet metal of the car. He bit his lip as he fought the pain in his chest.

As they accelerated past the Mexican side of the border, Bill slung the empty Uzi at a slow-moving Mexican, striking him in the head. They roared through the gate and under the awning on the American side, narrowly missing the guardhouse on their left. Most of the American officials huddled in the brick building on their right, out of harm's way. As the Challenger shot by them, several men stepped into the roadway, pistols drawn. Bill saw one of the men pull a man's pistol down. *Good ol' Oscar -- he recognized me. I told him someday I'd come back for Freddy.* He shook his head to fight off the pain.

From the back seat, he heard Mike's voice. "Ha! We made it! We fuckin' made it!"

In the rearview mirror, Bill saw him pop his head up and look into the front seat. "Oh, shit! Oh shit! Oh shit! Oh, my god!"

Bill glanced at the passenger seat. Frederico's face was unidentifiable. Something had hit him in the head. It didn't matter now. His body lay slumped against the door, his brains running down the door panel.

Bill blinked his eyes to focus them.

"Oh, shit! Pull this thing over, man. You're hit bad," said Mike.

Julie looked at him in the mirror. He saw her eyes go to Frederico, then she sat up and peeked over his shoulder. "You're bleeding to death, Bounty Hunter. My god, stop the car!"

Bill clenched his teeth. "Not till we hit Tucson, Peaches."

"Peaches? Peaches! You're bleeding to death and you sit there and make up nicknames? What the hell kind of person are you?"

Bill held the wheel with his right hand, his left pressing hard against the hole in the upper right side of his chest. "Can you stop the bleeding? I'm losing ground."

"Damnit, you stop this car!"

"Sorry."

She crawled over the back of the seat and squeezed between him and Frederico's body, her bare legs grinding broken glass into the seat and into her skin. She moved his hand and pressed both of hers against the wound. Blood spurted into her face. Her hands slipped from the wound and she quickly replaced them. "Stop the car damnit! You're going to bleed to death behind that goddamn wheel! This is crazy!"

"Not yet."

"When? When you're dead?"

"We've gotta get by Bisbee and on the road to Saint David."

"How much further is that?" asked Mike.

"Just a few more minutes."

"Slow this thing down, man, there's nobody following us." said Mike.

"They may have radioed to the Cochise County Sheriff."

"So what? Isn't that what you wanted?" asked Julie.

Bill shook his head. "If they get me, there's a chance I'll be extradited back to Mexico for murder."

"You're kidding? But those guys were trying to kill us," said Mike.

"Proving it in a Mexican court is not something I look forward to -- besides, have you forgotten about that police car? We don't know what happened to the cops inside it."

"You mean you're a bona fide criminal, just like us now, huh?"

"I guess, Mike. I guess," said Bill tiredly.

Bill slowed for the left turn at the junction of

Highway 89 and gunned the big engine up the slight grade and through the canyon, rumbling into the open plain on the west side of the hills.

"You're still losing blood, Bounty Hunter. I can't stop it all. It's leaking by my fingers."

Bill took his eyes off the road long enough to form a picture of Julie, her face covered with his blood, her own legs bleeding from the cuts inflicted by the broken glass on the seat, her hands soaked in red from her fingers to her elbows. He shot another glance at Frederico's body, then returned his attention to the road.

South of Saint David, he turned the car off the road, into a grove of cottonwood trees and shut off the engine. "Get the pressure bandage out of the first aid kit."

Julie was near hysteria. "I can't! Don't you understand, you hardheaded bastard? You'll bleed to death damnit!"

"Maybe I can get it." Mike fished in the pack with his hands cuffed behind his back until he was able to extract the kit. He bent forward, facing the back of the car and handed it over the seat to Julie, who managed to remove one of her hands from the wound long enough to accept it.

"Do you know how to apply one of those?" asked Bill.

"Don't give me a lecture right now, Bounty Hunter. I'm not in the mood."

She ripped his shirt at the shoulder, ignoring the blood as it spurted onto her blouse. She fumbled with the bandage, whimpering in desperation as she tore it from its sterile wrapping. Quickly, she jammed it over the wound. She rested for a moment, then, with her free hand, she picked up the roll of adhesive tape and applied it liberally to the bandage. When it was secure enough to remain in place, she used both hands to wrap it tightly to him, around his chest and up over his shoulder. When she completed her task, she leaned back against the dash and surveyed her work.

"Thanks," said Bill quietly.

Julie blew a strand of bloody hair from her eyes. "What happened to 'Peaches'?"

"You didn't like it."

"I like it now."

Her blouse was soaked. It clung to her body like she had just been in some sadistic blood-wet-t-shirt contest. Her face was painted red like the fiercest of the plains Indians must have looked when they made war. Her hair was a sticky mass of coagulating blood, darkening rapidly in drying chunks.

Bill started the engine. "You're kinda cute."

She looked at him quizzically.

He put the Challenger into gear and pulled onto the highway, less hurried now, less desperate, more confident, weaker. "You okay back there, Mike?"

"Don't you get tired of asking that question? If we'd got caught by a more sane bounty hunter, none of this would be happening. Christ, we'd probably have been better off in the hands of the Mexican police."

"You don't believe that."

"Naw, but at least it would have been a quicker way to die. This doing it in stages is wearing me a little thin. I keep waitin' for the end to come. I know damn good 'n well, if we stay with you long enough, it will."

"Maybe you're right there, Mike. Maybe you're

right."

"Look, man, you've proved your point. You got us. Now, what say you turn us loose for a cool half million?"

"I gotta hand it to you, Mike, you don't give up all that easy." Bill felt weak and suffered dizziness. He shook it off.

"What about him?" Julie was facing forward now, her hips against Frederico's slumped back, wiping at the small cuts on her legs.

"We'll get rid of him up here on the other side of Benson. I'll call the Cochise County Sheriff when we get to Tucson."

Julie shuddered. "Just like that -- and he's dead."

"You miss him? I don't."

"No, but he was still a human being."

"No he wasn't."

"You don't really mean that?"

He looked at her bleeding legs. "You had really pretty legs before we started this trip. I guess I haven't been too good for you have I?"

"They'll heal. Only a few of them are deep enough to leave scars, and they won't be too bad."

"I like your attitude."

"Yeah, well, what about mine?" asked Mike.

Bill looked at him in the mirror. "For murderers, you're both all right. Sorry about having to keep you cuffed, Mike, but you're behind me. I'll get them off of you as soon as I can."

"Don't do me any favors."

They rolled into Benson and Bill slowed the car to the speed limit. A city police car sat at the side of the road on the west end of town, its driver issuing a traffic citation to the driver of late model Ford pickup. Bill held his breath as they drove by the cruiser uncontested. The officer hadn't even looked up at the passing car. If he had, the broken windshield would have been more than ample reason for a traffic stop. They passed under Interstate 10 and hit the on-ramp up the big hill on the west side of town. Bill took the car up to seventy miles per hour and held it comfortably at that speed.

At the top of the hill, he noticed the temperature gauge beginning to climb. "Nuts!"

"Nuts?" said Mike from the back seat.

"The engine is heating up. Something must have got hit when we crossed the border."

Bill watched Mike in the mirror as he looked around the car, then nodded. "Yeah, I'd say something got hit all right -- about everything in, on, or around this car for starters."

Bill topped the hill and slowed the car down to fifty miles per hour. The gauge stopped climbing. He made the decision to continue to the small store and gas station only a mile or two up the road. He knew he'd made the wrong decision when he glanced at the oil pressure gauge and saw the needle wavering near zero. He pulled the car off the roadway and through the grass, up against the fence marking the freeway right of way. Just as he turned the key off, one of the connecting rods snapped with a resounding crash. Bill hit the steering wheel with his left hand, the movement causing pain in his chest and shoulder.

"What the hell was that?" asked Mike.

"The engine just committed suicide," answered Bill.

"Jesus Christ! Nothing lives long around you.

You're a goddamn jinx, you know that?"

Bill shook his head and closed his eyes. "Not now, Mike. Not now, okay?"

"What do we do now, Bounty Hunter?"

Bill sat silently for a moment. He wanted to cry out of frustration, but that wouldn't appear very macho to his prisoners. He fought off the urge. "We catch a train."

"We do what?" said Mike.

"We catch a train. About a mile or so north of here, the Southern Pacific should have a long freight rolling through here in about an hour or so. If we get started right away, we'll make it with time to spare."

"I hate to remind you of this, but you're shot -- my hands are cuffed behind my back -- we got a dead man with us -- Julie is half crippled, and this is nineteen ninety-one. Nobody rides the rails anymore, man."

Bill looked at Mike and smiled. "Just think -- you can tell your grand kids you rode the rails in nineteen ninety-one. C'mon, let's go." He opened the door and held the seat forward for Mike, then put it back in place so Julie could get out. They picked up their gear, including the Uzi, and set off on foot, leaving Frederico's body in the car where he had died. Soon they were out of sight of the freeway.

Bill carried the weapons and found the weight too much for him. He extracted the magazine from the Uzi and handed it to Julie. He uncuffed Mike and gave the gun to him. "Mike, you walk in front, Julie next. Don't get within ten feet of each other. I didn't come this far to have you blow me away."

Mike put a hurt expression on his face. "The thought would never cross my mind."

Bill smiled weakly. "I know, but it's like reading you your rights. You've got the right to die if you do think about it too seriously. I just think it only right that you know these things. Now, let's get moving."

Mike stepped out in a low crouch, the Uzi at high port arms, imitating a soldier crossing an open battlefield. Bill laughed, sending a jolt of pain through his body. He fought it off. "Hey, Mike, were you ever in the service?"

He stood erect and turned his head as he continued to walk. "Do I look that stupid?"

Bill shook his head. "Yes, but I take it that means you weren't."

"You take it right, man. I don't like guns. They hurt people."

"Yeah, sometimes they even hurt the right people."

Mike trudged on, silently.

The railroad tracks appeared in the large canyon below as they rounded a small hill.

"Hey, Bounty Hunter, what are you going to do with all of that money?" panted Julie as she hobbled ahead of him, aided by the support of a large mesquite branch.

"Look for another '69 GTO convertible with a ram air IV engine and a four speed."

"Doesn't seem like you come out much ahead if that's all you get out of it."

"Oh, I'll make a few house payments and catch up on my bills. I'll be just fine, don't you worry your pretty little head about me."

She turned her head and pouted. "I just wondered what a person like you does with his money."

"There *is* no other person like him," said Mike from his point position.

"Thanks, Mike, I appreciate that."

"You're welcome."

They continued in silence.

They reached the tracks at the end of Bill's endurance. He sat on the ground and propped his back against a mesquite tree, out of breath. Julie stood near him, looking down.

"You okay?"

"I hate to disappoint you, but yeah, I'm fine."

"Quit being such a tough guy. It doesn't work. Let's try it again -- you all right?"

"I'm fine -- just fine. Now hand me that magazine and sit down or I'll cuff you until the train gets here. Mike, bring the Uzi over here and set it down."

"Aw, shucks, and just when I was beginning to have fun, too."

They sat silently and smoked cigarettes while they waited for the train. On his second cigarette, Mike said, "Isn't that train gonna be haulin' ass when it comes by here?"

Bill shook his head. "It slows quite a bit for this grade. It'll still be moving plenty fast, but we can jump it. I'll pick the car. We'll run up next to it, throw the gear into it, then you, then Julie then me." He looked at Mike and smiled. "I'll have the Walther in my hand, Mike, so don't go thinking silly thoughts."

"Darn -- caught me at it again."

The freight train could just be seen, puffing its way up the grade, on its way out of Benson. Bill looked at them. "Get ready. Get your gear in your hands and be ready to go."

Julie stamped out her cigarette nervously. "I can't

do it. There's no way I can do it."

"You'll do it, Peaches, or I'll throw you on it myself."

"It's getting closer, man. Jeez! Are you sure we'll be able to jump that thing? It looks awful fast to me."

"We can make it. Just do as I say." He studied the cars as they approached. "See that boxcar with the open door -- about the tenth car back? That's the one. Quick, let's hide so the engineer doesn't see us."

They hid near a group of creosote bushes as the four big diesel engines passed them. When he felt it was safe, Bill stepped up next to the track, pushing Mike and Julie before him. "C'mon, let's go! Start running, just as fast as you can. Throw the gear in -- now!"

Mike tossed in the pack and the Uzi, Julie threw in the canteen and Uzi magazine. Bill slid the M-1 onto the wooden floor as carefully as circumstances would allow. Mike was already fighting his way onto the high floor of the car. Bill grabbed the rear of the opened door and held on with his right hand. Julie hobbled next to the door, making no attempt to jump on board.

"Mike! Grab Julie's hand! Help her."

Mike reached out and latched onto her hand, bracing himself with his other hand on the inside of the car as he pulled on her arm. Bill ran up behind her and lifted her quickly by the waist, physically throwing her onto the car. The bandage tore loose and he felt the blood rushing down his chest. He tried to grab the door again but there was no strength in his body. He felt the door slipping from his hand as the world went out of focus. His hand slipped away and he tumbled to the ground, rolling with his forward movement as he had been taught in boot camp. He came to rest in a creosote bush, its strong, clean odor jarring him into full consciousness for a few seconds as the train rolled by. It went out of focus. He put his left hand on the bandage and pressed. *What a way to end a life.* His world went black.

CHAPTER 11

"He's dead, damnit. We walked all the way back here for nothing." It was a male voice.

Bill felt hands searching him, removing the Walther from his waistband holster, the Smith from the belt holster. Other hands touched his face, tapping his cheeks lightly. "C'mon, Bounty Hunter -- be alive." This voice was female.

Bill opened his eyes and fluttered his eyelids, trying to focus. He knew it was Julie and Mike, but they were all fuzzy, out of shape.

"He's alive, Mike, damnit. He's alive."

"Great. Now we can look forward to meeting him again someday. Think about that, sis. This crazy bastard might try it again."

"Shut up, Mike. Quit trying to be macho." She nodded at Bill. "On him it's natural -- on you it doesn't fit. You know as well as I do we can't leave him here to die."

Mike rubbed the stubble of growth on his chin. "There's no doubt I'd be deader than ol' Freddy back there if he hadn't been in that bar with his damn gun that night.

"Peaches?" He saw her plainly, her face covered with dried blood -- his blood.

She smiled, her teeth a bright white in contrast to the dark blood on her face. "I swear, I'm beginning to like you a little bit."

Bill tried to sit up. She pushed him back. "Whoa, take it easy."

"I'm just trying to get the wound above my heart."

Julie looked dumbly at Mike, who shrugged his shoulders. "I'm no doctor, but it makes sense to me," he said. "Besides, this guy's probably been shot so many times, he's got more experience than a doctor anyway." He knelt next to them and helped prop Bill up against the center of the creosote.

"Thanks," Bill said quietly.

"I owe you more, but that's all there is for now," said Mike as he looked at the wound.

"Be still. I've got to re-dress this thing," said Julie. She turned to Mike. "Hand me the first aid kit, will you?"

The initial shock of the torn flesh and muscle had long since worn off, and Bill suffered a lot of pain, both the strong, dull type and the sharp biting kind when he moved in certain ways. He winced involuntarily as Julie moved him a little to get a better position to work.

"Mike, hold him for me. Help."

Mike crawled into the creosote bush and held Bill's shoulders as Julie completed the removal of the old bandage and cleaned around the gaping hole with water from the canteen and a piece of her blouse tail.

"I wouldn't tear too much of that thing off -- you won't have anything left to wear." Bill smiled weakly.

Julie's eyes met his briefly. She returned to her work, gagging once or twice as she got too close to the deep purple hole in his chest with the damp cloth. Bright red blood dripped from the center of the dark purple in a steady stream, but it was not the heavy flow of earlier.

She stopped dabbing at the wound and looked at him, the corners of her mouth turned down.

"It doesn't look so good, Bounty Hunter."

Bill grinned. "To tell you the truth, it feels just like it looks."

Julie put a new bandage on the wound and taped it tightly. "The bullet must still be in there. I can't see where it came out."

Bill nodded. "It's in there all right -- I can feel it."

"Oh, jeez, man. Don't say that!" said Mike in his ear.

Julie looked around them. "What are we going to do?" She looked at Mike, then down at Bill. "If we don't get him to a doctor, he's going to die of infection or something. I don't know where that bullet is, or what it's tearing up right now."

"What the hell can we do? We can't carry him back up to the freeway -- it's too far and it's all up hill."

Julie looked at the bandage. "He'd never make it anyway."

"Don't be so sure." Bill sat weakly upright.

Mike backed out of the creosote and picked up the Uzi.

"Relax, Mike. Where's my M-1?"

"You mean that long-barreled cannon? It's layin' over there." He nodded. "Scratched up the stock a little bit when we jumped from the train, but it's here."

"Is that all you can think about -- a stupid gun?" asked Julie.

"Rifle," corrected Bill.

Julie stood. "Stop it, both of you! Quit talking about guns. I'm sick of guns! Damnit, I want out of here!

I never want to see another gun as long as I live. Just stop talking about them, okay?"

Bill looked at Mike and raised an eyebrow. Mike shrugged.

"Speaking of guns, there, man, what say you give me that knife?" Mike motioned to the sheath knife on Bill's belt.

"Sure. Just take care of it. It's a good piece of steel."

Mike placed the Uzi, barrel up, against a small palo verde tree and knelt in front of Bill to relieve him of the knife. Bill held his hands in his lap as Mike knelt over. When Mike reached out and unsnapped the loop on the sheath to remove the knife, Bill jammed his hand into Mike's throat and held it there. He could tell by Mike's eyes, the other man could feel the cold steel at his throat. "Don't move, Mike. Sit next to me, real slow.

Mike turned and sat slowly, Bill's hand still holding the metal object against his throat. Julie looked at them, a startled expression on her face. "Where did you get that thing? I thought we took all of your guns."

Bill smiled slyly at her. "I don't tell even you everything, Peaches."

"Is that thing real?" she asked.

All the while, Mike sat stiffly, not breathing, the derringer under his chin.

".357 magnum. Two shots. One for each of you, if I have to."

Julie kicked angrily at the ground. "We should have left you to die. It would have served you right."

Despite his predicament, Mike nodded slightly. Bill looked at him and took the derringer from his throat.

"Goddamnit, Julie, we were home free. We were outa here, but no, we had to come back to this money-hungry bastard. All we had . . ."

Bill backhanded him. "Your language."

"Ow!" Mike grabbed his mouth.

Julie laughed. "This is ridiculous. This whole scene is ridiculous. Everything is ridiculous." She sat facing Mike and Bill. "Okay, Mister Bounty Hunter, what now?"

"I need a favor."

"I'd say you need a bunch of favors from the looks of that wound, man," said Mike.

"I'm serious. I need you to trust me for a while. If you trust me, I'll trust you -- real simple."

"What are you talking about -- trust you? You got the gun."

"It doesn't matter, I wouldn't use it on either one of you. He tucked the derringer into the inside holster to the left of his fly.

Julie winced. "Aren't you afraid of an accident?"

Mike jumped up and made a move for the Uzi.

"Sit down, Mike. I don't think we need those guns anymore. If he was going to shoot us, he could have done it just now," said Julie.

Mike stopped mid-step at his sister's strong tone of voice, and sat next to her.

"Let's hear it, Bounty Hunter," said Julie.

"I need a doctor."

"No shit," said Mike.

Julie glanced sharply at him.

Bill continued, "If I go to a hospital, chances are good the authorities will figure out it was me who busted the border and from there they'll trace my trail back to Guaymas. I don't need that kind of trouble."

"You've got to have a doctor, man. I saw that hole in your chest. Christ, even I could drive a semi through it, and I can't drive a semi," said Mike.

"I could get by with an animal doctor."

"A veterinarian?" asked Julie.

"Not even a bona fide veterinarian, just a man who's doctored a lot of animals."

"Where you gonna find this guy?" asked Mike.

"The same place I'm gonna find a place for you to hide until your trial."

Mike rolled his eyes. "We're not back to that, are we?"

"I know you guys didn't kill anybody, and you said yourself, the Mexican Mafia only set you up to find you and blow you away. There's not enough evidence to convict, right?"

Julie nodded. "What are you getting at?"

"You can't run from the American law and the Mexican Mafia too. Oh, you can for a while, but it wouldn't be long before one side or the other was knockin' your door down. If you showed up for trial, the case would be dismissed; that takes care of one problem. At least you can live in this country anywhere you want without hiding from the law. If we show up at the hour of your trial, the Mexican mafia won't have much of a chance to do their work. I'll be right outside. We'll get an attorney and you'll be free in a matter of hours. I can make all of the arrangements."

"What's in it for you?" asked Julie.

"Probably nothing."

Mike stood. "Wait a minute. Whoa there, cowboy. You mean you expect us to believe that you're going to give up two-hundred thousand dollars, just like that?"

"It does sound kind of stupid, doesn't it?"

"Why?" asked Julie. She stared into his eyes.

"Cause I think you're telling me the truth, and it isn't worth two-hundred thousand dollars if I'm right. I don't want to see you both killed for my financial well-being."

"Are you serious?" asked Mike.

Julie continued to stare at him, tears starting to fill her eyes.

"Yeah," Bill sighed. "I'm serious."

"Who is this guy who's going to doctor you and hide us?"

"My dad."

"Your father?" repeated Mike. "You got a father? Hell, I thought you just appeared out of nowhere one day, fully-grown and carrying that damned M-1."

Bill grinned and nodded. "Him and my mother work a small ranch about fifteen miles southwest of here -- the Lazy R."

"Jesus! You mean you *are* a cowboy?" asked Mike.

"I know how to ride a horse, if that's what you mean. It's my dad and mother who work the ranch. I only help out during the roundups in the spring and fall."

"You'd take us to your parent's house?" asked Julie, tears now rolling down her cheeks.

"I don't think either one of us has much choice, if you think about it."

"How are we going to get you there?" she asked.

"Wait a minute, Julie. Think about this a minute.

Do you believe this guy -- even for one minute?"

She looked at Mike with a scowl, then at Bill. "I want to, so I do. He's telling us the truth -- I know he is."

Mike shrugged. "Okay, cowboy, how do we get you and Julie to this Lazy R place?"

"I'll draw you a map. You'll have to walk it. My dad's got a four-wheel drive pickup. He can get here in no time."

"Why should he believe me?"

"Just try telling the truth. He'll know if you're lying or not. Just in case that doesn't work, tell him I told you John Clum needs his help."

"John Clum needs his help?"

Bill nodded, causing a sharp pain to run down his chest.

"Jeez! You even got codes with your old man?"

"He might not even remember it, but years ago I told him if he ever got that message, whoever gave it to him was on the level."

"This is weird, man."

"Oh, yeah, be careful of Rufus."

"Rufus?"

"The dog. He's a Shepherd mix. Smarter'n most people. You won't be able to fool him either. Just promise him you'll take him hunting and he'll stand away from you until my father or mother gets to you. Just don't make any sudden moves, or attempt to go past the big mesquite in the front yard. Hail the house from there."

"This is getting worse." Mike looked at Julie. "Draw me that map. I might as well get this over with."

"My notebook is in my shirt pocket," said Bill.

Julie reached into the blood-soaked pocket and

withdrew a small notepad. She flipped several pages until she found one dry enough to use. She folded the page back and handed the pad to Bill, then removed the ballpoint pen from his pocket.

Bill thought for several long moments then began to draw lines on the page. After a short period, he offered the pad to Mike. "It's no masterpiece but it'll get you there."

With the rough map in his hand, Mike picked up the Uzi.

"What's that for?" asked Bill.

"It's so Rufus will know I'm not bullshittin' when I tell him I'll take him hunting later."

Bill smiled. "Get outa here. Oh, you might tell him to bring some food. I think Peaches here could use some."

"I'll be back just as soon as I can," said Mike over his shoulder as he set out for the southwest.

There was a long, awkward silence between them after Mike left. Finally, Bill said, "How's your ankle?"

"Lousy. How's your bullet wound?"

"Same."

Silence followed.

Julie rubbed the tears from her cheeks, smearing the dried blood. Bill smiled. "I wish I was fifteen or twenty years younger."

Julie looked at him, a serious expression on her face. "I do too, but you're not, so we'll just have to make do with what we have."

Bill shook his head. "I'll have to pass this time, Julie."

"What happened to Peaches?"

Bill shook his head. "Don't know. Guess I was getting too used to the name. When this is over -- if it ever is -- then we go our separate ways. I don't want to be yearning after some gal twenty years younger than me."

"'Yearning'? Did anyone ever tell you, you talk funny sometimes? I kind of like it, but it's a little of out of date."

"I'm out of date, kid, that's what I'm trying to tell you."

"I meant what I said that night you put your arm around me."

"Thanks. That's quite a compliment -- either that, or it doesn't say much for your boyfriends."

"Both, I guess."

"How did you and Mike ever get mixed up in this whole thing?"

"We knew someone, who knew someone, who knew someone. We went to the right parties in LA, then Mexico City, then Hermosillo."

"Where'd you get all this money to go to these places?"

She leaned close to him. "Don't talk anymore, Bounty Hunter." She put her lips on his and kissed him gently and long.

Bill made no move to resist the kiss. He wanted to kiss her. He wanted to hold her. But he didn't go that far. He just sat there and took the taste of her lips into his mouth. She gently searched the inside of his mouth with her tongue. He felt a stirring inside and pulled his head back. "Uh uh."

"Why? You didn't like it?"

"Just the opposite. It was just a sample and it was enough to let me know you're the girl I dreamed of -- twenty years ago."

She sat back on her haunches. "Damnit, Bounty Hunter, stop it! You're not that old. Quit making it sound like you're a hundred years old. I could tell by the kiss that you're a long way from being over the hill. It was good -- even better than I thought it would be."

"Forget it, Peaches. You and me are not an item. We could never be."

"Why? Because you think I'm a tramp?"

"No. I don't think you're a tramp."

"You too good for me?"

"Quite the contrary."

"You think I'm too good for you? That's a laugh."

"It's not a question of who's too good for whom. You're young, and you've got a lot of things to do with your life -- good things and bad things -- but you'll do all right."

"What if I want to do them with you?"

"You don't. You may think you do right now, but you don't."

"What makes you so damn smart? How come you think you know everything?"

"I've lived a long time and put on some fast miles. I don't know everything, but I know more than you do."

"Damnit." She stood and stomped her good foot on the ground. "Listen to me, Bounty Hunter -- what's your real name by the way?"

"Bill. Bill Rutledge."

"Bill? That's it? No 'Killer Kane' or 'Smokin' Sam'? Just plain old Bill?"

"Sorry to disappoint you."

She smiled. "I like it. I think it's great."

Bill coughed. He covered his mouth with his hand. When he pulled it away from his lips, it was covered with dark blood.

"Oh my God! You're bleeding internally! Why didn't you say something?"

"I'm getting cold, Peaches."

She put her hand on his forehead. "Oh God! You're ice cold. What do I do, Bounty Hunter?"

"Help me get propped up against that palo verde, then see if you can find something to cover me up with."

"What's a palo verde?" she asked.

He nodded. "That tree with the green bark."

"Oh." She grunted and groaned as she tugged and pulled at his shoulders, favoring her injured ankle, until she had him propped up against the palo verde. Bill suffered the pain she inflicted silently. She searched desperately for something to keep him warm. Nothing. She looked at her thin cotton blouse and untied the knot at the bottom.

Bill waved a hand feebly. "I appreciate the gesture, but that's a total waste of time." He smiled.

She re-tied the knot and looked at him. "Damn you, I'm not going to let you die. You'll be going into shock if we don't get you warm. I remember that much of my schooling."

Bill's teeth chattered. "I know, Peaches. I know."

Again she looked around. She limped up and down the small wash south of the tracks. When she returned to Bill, she was empty-handed and panting. "There's nothing. What am I going to do? I've got to do something, damnit. Help me!" She looked at the cloudless sky.

Suddenly, she walked to Bill and stooped next to him. She took the knife from his sheath.

Bill smiled weakly up at her through chattering teeth. "You gonna make it painless for me?"

"Shut up, damnit!" She knelt on one knee and cut the rest of his shirt away.

"I think you've got it wrong, Peaches. I need more cover, not less."

She didn't say a word as she peeled the tattered rag from his body, then untied her blouse and opened it. She was naked beneath it. She put her arms around him and held her body to his.

He felt her firm breast touch his chest, but experienced no male reaction. His only reaction was to the warmth of her body. He put one arm around her and pulled her closer. She reached out and grabbed the pack, placing it near the trunk of the palo verde, and laid his head gently upon it, then lay gently on him, most of her body weight on the ground, but her warm flesh covering his torso, clinging to it like a vine clings to a fencepost.

"If you're going to die, Bounty Hunter, do it now."

He kissed her forehead. "Sorry to disappoint you, but I think I'll stay around for the next act."

She squeezed him until he winced, then backed off her grip only slightly and hung on. "Damn you, Bill Rutledge. Damn you." She wept silently, her tears falling onto his lower neck.

Bill lay unmoving, thinking about all he could remember of his life, remembering nothing in its completeness, but rather seeing only glimpses here and there, unconnected events that built nothing, none adding to the other. He felt Julie's tears on his neck and her breath on his upper chest. He felt her warm skin against his. He felt his own pain, and a pain even greater than the physical. Sadness and sorrow swept over him -- sadness for what he knew could never be, and sorrow for those things in his life he could not -- would not change. He fell asleep to Julie's steady breathing.

CHAPTER 12

"Goddamnit! Every time I leave him alone with my sister, I find him sleeping with her."

Bill woke to Mike's voice. Julie stirred. She put her arms around his neck and hugged him.

"Julie, damnit, get up!"

She turned and looked up at her brother, her breasts exposed.

"Jesus. cover yourself. I got his father with me."

"I've seen it all before," said Bill's father disinterestedly.

"Julie, what the hell are you doing? I thought this guy was too hurt to move. I guess he's not to hurt for a little fun in the sun, huh?"

Julie stood and tied her blouse at the bottom, buttoned it almost to her neck, then walked to Mike and hit him in the mouth with a closed fist. He fell onto his back and looked up at her.

"Why'd you do that?"

She turned to Bill's father. "Hi. I'm Julie Short."

He glanced over his shoulder as he unloaded blankets from the bed of the pickup. "Sam Rutledge. Was he cold?"

"Yeah, how'd you know?"

"Looked to me like you were keeping him warm

real good." He glanced at Mike, still laying on the ground, propped up on his elbows. "Leastwise, I can't think of anything else you'd be doing with only the top half of you undressed."

Bill smiled as his father turned to him with several blankets in his hands. "Howdy, Bill. Looks like you bit off a mite much this time."

"Howdy, Dad. Yeah, but I think we can get it handled now."

Sam Rutledge knelt next to his son and removed the bandage.

"Where's Ma?"

"At the house -- gettin' things ready. You know how she is about company." He probed around the wound.

"You've lost a little of that gentle touch in your old age there, Dad." Bill winced.

"Sorry. Just had to see if I could figure which direction that thing went."

"I can answer that one for you. Did you bring your stuff?"

"In the truck. You reckon you can make it to the house?"

Bill shook his head. "To tell you the truth, I think the bullet is awful close to the lung. It must have got a piece of it or something. I coughed a little blood."

"Where's the slug?"

"There's a bump on my back, just below my shoulder blade. I think it wanted to come out, but it just didn't have the horsepower."

Sam lifted him gently and felt the bump. "Oh, yeah, I see it." He turned to Mike. "Say, Mike, you wanna give me a hand getting him to the bed of the truck?"

Mike, who stood sullenly next to Julie, jumped to Sam's side. "You just tell me what you want me to do."

"Grab his feet." He looked quickly at Julie. "Would you spread out a couple of blankets for me in the bed?"

Julie complied quickly, and soon Bill was lying on his stomach, his head at the rear of the bed. Sam probed the bump on his back.

"Yeah, I'd say it come right close to that lung. You really ought to go on into Tucson and have 'em pull it out proper."

"I can't, dad. Trust me on this one."

He furrowed his brow. "Okay. I'll get right to it." He stepped to the driver's door of the pickup.

Julie knelt at the back of the truck until Bill could meet her eyes. "What's he going to do?"

Bill was already feeling better. "He's gonna take that piece of lead outa me."

Julie's mouth fell open. "Right now? Here?"

"Now's as good a time as any -- better actually."

Sam stepped to the back of the truck, an old brown leather bag in his hand. The look on Julie's face was one of horror. She stepped in between Bill and his father. "No! You can't do this! This is crazy!"

"Yeah, you got that right," said Mike. "What he needs is a hospital and a surgeon."

Sam placed the bag at the back edge of the bed and said, "Seems like your girl doesn't want me to take that slug out." He rubbed his chin.

"Can you do it?" said Bill.

"It looks almost like it did it itself. All I gotta do is slice the skin and pull it out."

"Then do it."

"No!" Julie screamed as Sam opened the weather-beaten bag. She set her jaw and put her hands on Bill's shoulders behind her.

Sam looked into her eyes. He spoke to Bill though he continued to look at Julie. "It seems like she still doesn't want it done, Bill."

Bill spoke into the blanket under him. "Julie, do you know how many bullets my father has cut out of cattle over the years? Probably more than every surgeon in Tucson put together. Seems like when hunters don't find deer, some of them like to shoot cattle."

"It hasn't been so bad this past ten years though," offered Sam.

Julie hesitated. Reluctantly, she stepped to the side.

Sam pulled out a large syringe and needle.

"God! What's that for?" asked Mike.

"Whatever I need it for. Cattle usually." He knelt next to Bill's face and showed him the needle. "Sorry about the size. It's the only sterile one I have."

"Great." Bill clamped his teeth together and mumbled, "Let's get it done." He tensed his muscles in anticipation.

"You're gonna have to loosen up a bit, Bill," said his father.

"You know I can't stand needles."

Julie knelt behind the truck and put her face next to his. "You're afraid of needles?"

"I didn't say I was afraid of 'em. I just said I couldn't stand the things."

Mike got into the act. He crouched beside Julie

and looked into Bill's eyes with a smile. "You mean to tell me, after what I've just seen this past couple of days, that you're afraid of a little ol' needle?"

With his face buried in the blankets, Bill said, "Forget I mentioned it. Let's be done with it."

Almost instantly, he felt the stab of the needle and flinched involuntarily. Julie stood and held his shoulders gently. Bill felt the area around the lump burn in an ever-widening circle, the numb center of the circle expanding as the novocaine worked its way outward.

"Can you feel that?" asked Sam.

He felt the tapping of fingers on his back, but it was pressure he felt rather than the touch itself. "It's dead."

"Hold this bandage in place, will you, Mike?" said Sam. He knelt next to Julie's knees and smiled. In a pair of bloody tongs he held a flattened chunk of lead. "It came out clean."

"You got it already?" asked Bill, half expecting his father to be joking.

Sam's smile broadened. "It was easier than doctorin' a steer. Didn't have to fight through all that hair."

"I'll be damned," said Mike calmly.

Sam stood and removed the temporary bandage. He dropped sulfa powder into the wound and covered it with fresh gauze, then applied a fresh pressure bandage. When he was done, he said, "Let's get him to the house. That hole in his chest needs cleanin' real bad." He looked up at Julie, who still held Bill's shoulders loosely. "Would you mind riding in the back with him?"

"I had planned on it."

Bill rolled onto his back, and with their help, was able to turn and rest his head against the cab of the truck, cushioned by a layer of several blankets. Julie nestled next to him, careful not to disturb his position.

"You ready?"

Bill smiled weakly at his father. "Go for it."

He looked over at Julie as the truck moved slowly across the sand and brush, his father doing his best to miss as many of the bumps as possible. He smiled weakly. "Some grand finale, huh?"

Julie said nothing. She stared intently at him.

"Did I say something wrong?"

"How long did you say you were married?"

"I didn't, but it was about ten years."

"I'd like to meet the woman who could live through this for ten years. I've barely been at it for two days and I can't handle it."

"This sounds kind of corny, but how did you ever get mixed up in something like this? You or Mike either one. Neither of you seem the type."

She shrugged, careful not to touch him. "Spoiled brats, I guess. It was an exciting life -- or at least I thought it was until I met you -- now I know it was boring as hell." She glanced at the landscape behind the pickup. "It was all so superficial -- so glittery -- like Hollywood. All we did was party and have a good time. When we found out about this big drug deal, it seemed like an appropriate way to refill our coffers. I mean, we didn't look at it like we were stealing -- it was dirty money to begin with. We looked at it like we were doing the world and us a favor."

"Where'd you go to college?"

"What makes you think I went to college?"

"You try to hide it but it shows -- Mike too."

"I went to Berkeley. Mike went to Georgia Tech."

"Georgia Tech?"

Julie nodded. "You'd never know the guy had a degree in aerospace engineering."

"You two got everything in the world going for you. It just doesn't make sense to me why you'd do something so stupid."

"There's more, but you can't handle too much at once in your condition. Just lie still." She brushed his hair from his eyes.

Bill closed his eyes and felt the vibrations of the V-8 engine under the hood of the truck. He felt Julie's hand brush his forehead as she pushed the hair from his eyes. He thought of Laura and put her at his side in his mind. It was her brushing his hair back. It was her touching him and telling him she loved him. Her beautiful auburn hair stretched behind her in the wind as the pickup flew across the desert. There was no pain, only her touch, and that feminine smell that was Laura.

The truck rolled to a stop. He heard Rufus bark once, and opened his eyes to see the large, rust-colored dog standing at the rear of the truck, his fore paws in the bed. Bill smiled. "Rufus, you old rascal, how you been?"

The dog jumped into the bed and sat on the horizontal tailgate, looking at first Bill, then Julie. He cocked his head to one side and perked up his ears.

Bill said, "He smells the blood. And he's not quite sure if you caused it or not."

"Tell him I didn't have anything to do with it -- quick."

"It's okay, Rufus. Julie's a friend."

The dog stood and walked casually to Julie. She held herself rigid while he sniffed her once then sat between her and Bill. He put out a paw in Bill's direction. Bill took it in his left hand and shook it gently. "It's good to see you too, old man."

A shadow fell over them. Bill looked up into his mother's face. "Hi, Ma. How ya been?"

Frona Rutledge took a quick look at Bill, then a longer one at Julie. "Seems like I been better 'n you. It sure is hard to get you out here. Seems like you have to go to a bigger extreme every time we see you lately." Her lips were in the shape of a smile, but the worry in her eyes was not concealed.

"Ma, this young lady next to me is Julie Short. Julie, this is my mother, Frona Rutledge. Ma, Julie here could use a bath and something to eat, and some rest too, I reckon. Mike too."

Frona held out her hand to Julie, then climbed up into the bed of the truck and examined her son. "Damnit, Bill, this is serious this time. We've got to get his thing cleaned up right now."

"Oh, Ma, take it easy. It's not that bad." Her face began to spin over him. A yellow glare obliterated her from view, then blackness fell over him like a heavy curtain.

Bill awoke to the smell of cooking beef. Despite the pain in his chest and back, his mouth moistened at the thought of a tender juicy steak. He lay quietly in bed, in the room he had called his own for many years while growing up. He caught glimpses of conversation from the adjacent living room and listened intently while his father told stories of ranch life. Every once in a while, Mike or Julie said a few words and started him up on another story.

Bill smiled as his father spoke in that soft southwestern drawl of his and told of Bill's first roundup and about how he had run from the campfire when he found out the cowboys were preparing "mountain oysters" for supper. Everyone laughed at the punch line, including Sam.

"Your son is quite a guy, Mrs. Rutledge." It was Julie's voice.

"I told you to call me Frona. Yeah, he sure is. Coulda been a doctor, lawyer, or whatever else he wanted to be. I'll never understand him I guess." There was a pause. "It don't really matter though. He's as much a man as any ten doctors I ever met. And I won't even compare him to a lawyer."

Mike said something Bill couldn't hear, then he heard his mother's voice again. "Now that you've got all cleaned up, and we've got a few minutes before supper, you want to tell us what's going on? You don't have to of course, but I'm kinda curious."

"Frona!" said Sam.

"Well, damnit, Sam, they don't have to say anything if they won't want to."

"If it's all the same to you, I'd rather Bill told you when he wakes up," said Julie. "Shouldn't we check on him again?"

"Mercy, girl, you just checked on him ten minutes ago. He'll be all right. That wound cleaned up pretty good. The only thing that worries me a little is what he might have got in the way of internal injuries. Oh, shoot, go ahead and peek in on him. It won't hurt anything I guess."

Bill watched her walk into his darkened room. Her hair was clean and flaxen as it hung limply down her back. She wore a pair of his mother's Levis and a white cotton blouse. No makeup. The denims were a little loose, but the blouse was a perfect fit. He smiled at her as she approached the bed and peeked down at him. "You look nice, Peaches."

She beamed. "You think so?" She spun around slowly. "You think this is me, huh?"

"I think probably anything you wear is you. You've got the natural beauty to carry it."

She scooted a small chair next to the bed and sat. "How do you feel?"

"Stupid. And sore. And helpless. Did you remember to bring the M-1?"

"That big gun?"

"Yeah."

"Mike brought it. If it was up to me, we wouldn't have brought any of them."

"Well, bless Mike's heart. You getting on with my folks?"

She smiled. "I feel more at home here than I did at home."

"Good. My mother is a bit on the rough side at times, but she's all bark and no bite."

"I think she's great."

"She'll do."

"She sure looks young to have a son your..."

"My age? Yeah, she was only eighteen when I was born. My father too."

"I didn't mean it that way. All I meant was...well..."

"It doesn't matter." He smiled.

Julie lowered her voice. "Damn you, Bounty Hunter, you try to bring that age crap up and twist it into something that isn't there every time you get a chance. If you weren't hurt so bad, I'd show you how young you really are."

He reached out his hand and she took it in hers. "Listen, Peaches. It's been fun and all of that, but let's don't go any further down the road. I think you and Mike are okay -- best bounties I ever took into custody -- but let's let it go at that, okay?" It wasn't what he wanted to say, but her youthful beauty made him say it.

She leaned close to him and whispered. "No, we're not going to let it go at that. You've met your match this time, mister." She smiled and pecked him on the cheek with her lips. "I think supper is almost ready. I'll check on it and be back in a minute."

When she left the room, Bill's thoughts were a jumbled mass of beefsteak, Laura and Julie. His life had sure gotten complicated lately.

Two or three minutes later, Julie walked in with a steaming bowl of soup on a large tray. She placed it carefully over him and sat in the chair next to the bed. Bill looked at the soup, then at her. "What's this?"

"Hot soup. What does it look like?"

"Hot soup? I don't eat soup. I can smell beef cooking in there somewhere. I'll wait."

"Doctor's orders. You get nothing but soup for a while."

"What doctor?"

"Your mother."

"Oh, for crying out... You tell her I need some real food. We didn't get much to eat there for a while."

Julie shook her head, obviously enjoying her position of power. "You either eat the soup or you get nothing."

"Great. I can starve to death after all of this."

"Suit yourself."

He looked again at the steaming bowl. "What kind of soup is it?"

"Beef and vegetables."

Reluctantly, he picked up the spoon. Julie propped him up on several pillows and left the room, promising to return as soon as the rest of them were finished eating.

CHAPTER 13

　　　　Bill tried a few bites of the soup but found his appetite only a facade. As the effects of the novocaine wore off, a dull ache enveloped his body. Propped up in the pillows, the dullness of the ache sharpened in his chest. One of his ribs caused him extreme pain when he tried to breathe too deeply. He tried breathing deeply several times just to see whether or not the pain would go away but it only worsened with each breath.
　　　　Mike walked into the room and sat in the chair Julie had so recently vacated. "How you feeling?"
　　　　"Just great," Bill said weakly. "Just great."
　　　　Mike looked around the room nervously. "Look, man, I just wanted to say thanks. I can't believe you brought us here -- you know what I mean?"
　　　　"I speak English, so I guess I understand what you're sayin'. It's no big deal."
　　　　"No big deal? Hell, I wouldn't even think of trying this with my parents."
　　　　"People are different, Mike. That don't mean they're good or bad. It just means they're different."
　　　　Mike leaned closer. "I don't understand you, man. You're about the meanest son-of-a-bitch I ever met, pound for pound, and yet you talk like some kind of philosopher. What's your story?"
　　　　"When did you become so interested in people,

Mike?"

Mike glanced out the open window. "Since I met you, I guess -- that and all the bullshit we went through in so short a period of time. It seems like I've lived a thousand years. I feel that much older and smarter -- and damned lucky to be alive.

"I mean, look how this whole thing got changed around. You arrested us -- hell, you shot two guys before I even knew what the hell was going on -- then you shot a bunch more. Then that thing, when Julie twisted her ankle, then driving into those guys at the border. Then..."

"Mike, get to the point. I'm gettin' tired."

"Well, it's just that I never would have figured something like this."

"Like what?"

Mike looked around the room. "This. This house. Your parents. Instead of turning us in and collecting a fat reward, you hide us and feed us. I can't get over it." He narrowed his eyes. "This isn't some kind of trick is it?"

"Go eat. You been reading too many comic books and watching too much TV." Bill was asleep before Mike was out of the room.

A bright light and brighter voice jarred Bill out of a sound sleep. He turned his head and saw Julie opening the curtains in his room.

"What time is it?" he asked.

"Well. Good morning to you too," she said around a pleasant smile.

"Oh. I'm sorry. Good morning. What time is it?"

"About seven."

"Oh. Okay. Did you sleep well?"

She sat carefully on the bed next to him. "I never have any trouble sleeping around here. I'm so tired by the end of the day that I crash and burn by an hour after dark. Your folks are teaching us all about ranching and cattle and all of the other stuff that goes on out here. Did you know that the hills around here are a veritable jungle of wildlife? And that Rufus -- I've never seen a dog like him. He goes everywhere we go and he herds and cuts cattle better than a cowboy at the rodeo. I think he'd rather herd cattle than eat."

"What did you say?"

"I said…"

"Never mind. How long have we been here?"

"More than a week -- eight or nine days I think. I've lost track of time." She looked into his eyes. "I never want to leave this place, Bounty Hunter."

"A week!" He sat up, causing himself a considerable amount of pain. He grunted involuntarily. "Where have I been? What happened?" Vague, almost dream-like, images of his father and Julie cleaning his wound flashed through his consciousness.

Her look grew serious. "You were awake off and on most of the time. Of course, sometimes you talked crazy, but we all figured it was because of the fever." She put her hand on his forehead and smiled. "Looks like your father was right. He said you should beat it by today."

"A week?"

"Nine days I think."

"Oh no. I've got to get to a phone."

Julie pushed him back into the bed gently. "Not yet. Your father says you shouldn't move around for at least another week or two except for when we clean your wound -- that's twice a day in case you don't remember."

"I've got to make a call. If I don't, this is all for nothing. We can still make your court date without a hitch and get this over with if I can contact the right people."

"Can't we make the call for you?"

Bill shook his head. "Too risky. Where's my mother?"

"Out back I think. You want me to get her?"

He nodded. "Please."

In a few minutes, Frona Rutledge walked into the room, a concerned smile on her lips. "How you feelin' today?"

"I feel pretty good, but I can't remember much of anything since I've been here."

She sat in the ever-present chair at his bedside. "You've had a rough time of it this past week or so. Julie tells me you wanted to see me."

He knew his mother, and he could tell by the way she said Julie's name that she liked her. He found that strange, since what he knew of Julie wouldn't exactly put her at the top of his mother's lists of favorite persons. "How are her and Mike doing?"

"You wouldn't believe it. Dad's gonna make regular cowboys out of both of them in no time. That Mike is a good hand with a rope already -- and you ought to see Julie ride. It's like she was born to the saddle. They've really been a big help. Mike helped dad fix a broken pipe under the house, and Julie is taking care of all the work around here. I can't believe it. It's almost like being on vacation."

"I'm glad to hear that, Ma. I know you can use the help."

A concerned look furrowed her brow. "What are you going to do about them, son?"

"I'd like to hide them here until the trial date. I'm sure they'll be released. After that, they're on their own."

"What about Julie?"

"What about her?"

"I think she loves you. She sure asks a lot of questions. And whenever she says your name, it's got 'love' written all over it."

"I'm old enough to be her father."

"She said you'd say that."

"Well, I am."

"She's twenty-seven."

"That's still too young."

Frona's eyes met his and locked in. "The important thing is -- how do *you* feel about *her*?"

"Oh, Ma, I've got business to take care of. I think you've grown a little too fond of her myself."

"I think you better examine your own feelings and not be so worried about mine. I know you. This girl's got under your skin." She winked. "She sure is a looker."

"Ma, quit it, will you? I need you or dad to make a call to a friend of mine in Tucson. His name is Tom Lassiter. Tell him the situation and tell him to contact..."

At supper that evening, Bill sat at the table with the others, uncomfortable but happy to be alive and able to eat real food. Mike wore a clean denim work shirt and a new pair of Levis Sam had purchased for him in Benson. He looked healthy and happy. Julie too had on a new pair of Levis and a white cotton shirt. Her skin had bronzed and her hair had grown lighter. She looked as content as any woman Bill had ever seen. Who would have guessed that the life of a cowboy would suit either of these two?

"Pass the salt please," said Bill.

Julie intercepted the salt shaker. "You shouldn't have too much of this," she said as she handed the shaker to him. She sat on his right. Mike sat across from them, with Sam and Frona at either end of the table.

Sam buried his eyes in the food on his plate and smiled at Julie's remark.

Mike looked at her quizzically.

Frona said, "You might want to pay attention to what Julie says, Bill."

Bill looked at his mother, a mock grimace on his face. "I thought my problem was a bullet wound, not hardening of the arteries."

Julie said, "Well, Bounty Hunter, you *are* getting up there in years. One can't be too careful at your age, you know."

Bill cocked his head and gave her a hard look. "Really? Is that all for now, Doctor, or do you have more free medical advice you want to dispense?"

Mike said, "This is sure good roast beef, Mrs. Rutelege."

"Thank you, Mike. Eat all you want. There's plenty. You might want to save a little room for some apple pie though."

Mike, who was in the process of putting more beef and potatoes on his plate, held the spoon in midair a moment then decided that what he had already put there was enough, and he put his plate down in front of him and the spoon back in the bowl. "Apple pie, huh?"

"Dutch apple pie," said Frona.

"I'm sure glad you gave me the heads up on that one. I was about to fill the tank on beef, beans and potatoes."

Frona smiled and Sam chuckled. Julie said, "You know we have desert of some kind every evening."

"Yeah, but the food's so good, I need to be reminded to save a little room."

Bill chewed slowly on a piece of roast, swallowed it, then took a small bite of pinto beans. It was the first solid meal he could remember eating in the last ten days.

Bill sat in a rocker in the shade of the front porch, chewing a toothpick, watching Julie and Mike brand a calf in the coral. The two worked well as a team. Mike held his knee on the tied animal's body while Julie snatched the hot iron from the fire. She wrinkled her nose as the hot metal seared the flesh. Quickly she removed the iron and stepped back while Mike untied the hooves and let the frightened animal to its feet.

There were a lot of things about Julie to like. Besides her beauty, she had education, intelligence, wit, a sense of humor; she wasn't afraid of hard work, and she seemed happy living on the ranch. Bill shook his head.

It had been three days since his mother had driven into Benson and made the call to Tom, who had promised to drive out to the ranch within four days with details of the response to Bill's requests. Bill looked past the old mesquite in front of the house and down the narrow dirt road that led to the highway, half expecting to see Tom's '57 Chevy rumbling up to the house.

Mike and Julie climbed the corral fence and walked to the porch. Mike leaned against the rail and Julie sat on the steps.

"Whew!" said Mike. "Where's all the romance and stuff? This cowboyin' isn't what I see in the movies."

"You guys want some ice tea?" called Frona from inside the house.

"Love it," answered Julie with a smile at Bill. "You look pretty good today."

Bill smiled. "You don't look so bad yourself, 'cept for that smudge on your cheek."

Self-consciously, she wiped her cheek with the back of her hand, enlarging the smudge. Mike laughed. "Oh, yeah, that's much better."

Julie flashed white teeth in a broad smile. Bill shook his head. "Lean over a little."

She leaned close and he rubbed her cheek until the smudge disappeared. He was still daubing her cheek with a bandana when Tom's Chevy rolled under the old mesquite and stopped at the edge of the porch.

Bill's heart thumped heavily as he saw Laura in the passenger seat, her copper curls glistening in the midday sun. Unconsciously, he quickly leaned away from Julie and smiled. "Howdy." He looked into Laura's eyes and said, "I never expected to see you again."

"I think you were about to explain something to me when things started to happen real fast down in Guaymas. I'm anxious to hear what it was." She looked Julie over quickly and discreetly. Julie stared at her unabashedly.

Tom got out of the car and met Laura next to the porch. Bill said, "Mike, Julie, I'd like you to meet two very good friends, Tom and Laura. This is Julie and her brother Mike."

Tom shook hands with both of them, unable to take

his eyes from Julie, even while he shook Mike's hand. Bill felt a twinge of jealousy. Laura smiled as she shook Mike's hand and seemed uncomfortable when she took Julie's. Julie stared long and hard at her as they shook hands. *A little too long*, thought Bill.

Frona came from the kitchen with a large tray full of tall glasses of iced tea. The introductions were repeated and they settled comfortably on chairs and porch railing to enjoy the coolness of the tea and make small talk for a few moments.

It was Bill who ended the small talk. "So, what did Bernie say?"

Tom looked at the women and his face turned red. "He wanted to know who in the hell you thought you were -- and I promise you, those aren't his exact words -- but if you get them to LA for the court date, you still get the bounty and Mike and Julie here stand trial. This Bernie guy is something else. Anyway, he's got a friend, who's got a friend, who says if they show up, the State is going to drop the charges. They don't have enough to go to trial."

Bill smiled. "There's two pieces of good news."

Tom looked around the yard. "Hey, where's your GTO?"

Bill shook his head. "It died in Mexico. We sort of cremated it."

"Oh. That's too bad. That was a neat car."

"God, Tom. They barely got back with their lives and you talk about a car? I don't think I'll ever understand you," said Laura.

"That's okay, Laura. I'm proud he asked about the car. It *was* a great car, and Tom appreciates those kinds of things."

Julie warmed up to Laura for the first time. "I'm with you. There we were, getting shot at and chased and everything else you can think of, and he's worried about his car. I couldn't believe it."

"I guess these two are a lot alike." Laura nodded at Tom and Bill.

Julie seemed to stiffen. "Maybe about some things, but I never saw a man do what I saw Bill do when he was bringing us back to the States." Bill thought he heard a jealous pride in her voice. She even used his given name. He dismissed it.

Sam rode into the yard and dismounted, tying his bay to the coral fence. He plopped down on the porch and joined the conversation, which immediately turned to ranch work. After a few minutes, Bill stood shakily and asked Laura to join him in a short walk.

Julie looked up at him as he stood near her, the corners of her eyes drooping. He hadn't walked beyond the porch since getting out of bed. "Are you sure you feel strong enough to walk?"

Bill nodded. "I feel pretty good today. Nothin' but good news is comin' my way. It makes a man feel stronger in a hurry."

She looked away as Laura put her arm in his and they stepped off the porch and walked towards the coral.

"She's beautiful," said Laura softly as they approached the fence.

"She's pretty. And she's sexy. And she's smart. And she didn't kill anybody."

There was a short silence as Bill threw his arms over the upper rail on the coral. He suppressed a grunt.

Laura put her back to a post and cocked her head to one side. "You're a hard man to read, Bill."

"What's to read?" He didn't know what else to say.

"I had a great time in Guaymas."

He looked across the coral. "So did I -- until the shooting started. I'm sorry about that. And I wasn't doing what it looked like with that girl in the bar. I was just getting information from her about Mike."

Laura smiled. "I realized that later -- at least I thought I did."

Bill looked down at her. "It's good to see you, Laura. I didn't think I ever would again."

"Was it that bad down there?"

"No, not that. I was talking about the way we parted company. I didn't figure you'd let me get close enough to explain."

"Tom and I had a long talk that night. We looked all over town for you until after sunrise. I thought something terrible had happened to you and I'd never get to tell you that I understood."

"You do?"

"A little. Not everything, but a little." She glanced briefly at the porch. "It's hard to dislike her."

Bill smiled. "You shoulda been with us in the beginning -- you'd of found it a lot easier."

"She loves you. You know that, don't you?"

"What is it with women? I go along for years without a bunch of emotional attachment, and all of a sudden -- you tell me some girl loves me."

"She's no girl, Bill. She's as much a woman as I've ever seen. And she's in love with you. I know it's not my place to say anything, I mean, after all, you don't owe me anything, but I care. I would like to have had more time to get to know you. I've never heard Tom speak more highly of anyone in my life. And at least the first part of my trip to Mexico was one of the happiest times of my life." She sighed. "I guess I had just hoped for more."

"What are you talking about? She's a bounty, for cryin' out loud."

Laura glanced in the direction of the porch. "I should say so -- and then some." She looked back up at him. "I just wanted you to know that when it's all over, if you feel like it, I'd like to hear from you -- either way it goes."

Bill looked into her deep-green eyes. "Laura, there's nothing to wait for. After I get back in shape, and deliver them to LA, I'd like to go out with you. I don't need to wait for anything to know that."

She touched his arm. "Bill, you don't know how much I'd like to see you again, but I don't want to hear anything until it's all over. I want you to be sure."

"Laura, this is ridiculous. I'm a grown man. I ought to . . ."

She put a finger to his lips. "Let's go back to the porch. I've monopolized you as long as I'm going to." She put her arm in his and stepped out slowly.

"You sure look healthy to me for a guy who took a bullet in the chest," said Tom as they took their positions on the porch.

"I'm tough -- remember?"

Tom laughed. "I see they didn't take any of the fire out of you."

"Did you take care of the details?" asked Bill.

"As much as I could."

"What does that mean?" asked Julie.

"Well, old Bernie asked a few questions I couldn't answer."

"Like what?"

"I don't remember. I told him to write them down and mail them to me."

"You what?"

"Don't worry. I gave him my business address. He doesn't know what I look like, much less where I live. You're safe."

Bill felt a wave of uneasiness pass through his body. "I don't know, Tom. This Bernie didn't get to be one of the biggest bondsmen in LA by being stupid."

"Don't worry. It's all right. Even if he found you, what's he going to do? He's on your side, right?"

Bill nodded. "Yeah, but I don't know the guy personally, and I'd feel better if no one knew anything more than what I told you to tell him. He's contacting the public defender, right?"

"He said he'd contact their lawyer -- some guy named Bartlett."

"Casey Bartlett?"

"Yeah, that's it. How'd you know that?"

"He's one of the most famous criminal defense lawyers in the country. I can't believe they'd appoint him to act as defense counsel, even in a murder case. The guy is too busy." He looked up at Mike. "Nothing but the best for you two, it looks like."

Mike smiled weakly.

Bill looked back at Tom. "So, everything is set then, right?"

Tom stood and walked to his Chevy. "Yeah, but

I've got that list of questions. Ol' Bernie sent it special delivery." He pulled a large, bright-green envelope from the seat of the car.

Bill felt a heavy thumping in his chest. "Is that the envelope he sent it in?"

Tom nodded. "Yeah. I thought it was over-kill myself. It's twice as big as it needs to be -- and that color -- have you ever seen anything like it?" He smiled as he handed the envelope to Bill.

"Tom, I think you and Laura better leave now."

"What? You tired of our company already?"

Laura's brow furrowed.

Mike and Julie looked at him with raised eyebrows.

"It's the oldest trick in the world. He sends you the stuff in an envelope too big to put into a briefcase, and he makes it a color that can be spotted a hundred yards away. You've been had, Tom. Bernie knows where we are. He's had you followed."

Tom looked around nervously.

"Just act normal. Shake my hand like our business is over, then you and Laura get in the car and go home."

"But what about you?" asked Tom.

"I'm not worried about me. It's Julie and Mike he wants."

"You'll need help if he comes to get them."

"I don't think he'll come after them right away. He probably only had two guys tailing you. Now that he knows where they are, one of them will go after help -- or he may be content to just sit tight and keep an eye on 'em. I just don't want you here in case he wants to come after them. If he thinks you're going to be here, he'll just bring that many more men. I'd rather you left now."

Tom stood and shook Bill's hand slowly and deliberately. "God, Bill, I didn't have any idea. I'm sorry, man."

Bill grasped his friend's hand and shook it firmly. "Don't sweat it, Tom. It's done and over with. Let me take it from here. You don't think I'm going to let ol' Bernie cheat me out of two-hundred thousand dollars, do you?"

Laura hugged him gently. "Take care of yourself, Bill."

"Count on it," he said, a grin plastered on his lips. Her body felt good against his, no matter how brief the encounter. She smelled clean, womanly.

They waited on the porch until Tom's Chevy was out of sight, then drifted into the house, one by one. In the living room, Sam said, "Sounds to me like it might be time to make a move. What do you think?"

"Sounds like a plan to me, Dad. How about that old line cabin on the south boundary?"

"I'll gather up some grub and vitals and have it ready by tonight," said Frona.

"I'll saddle the horses after dark, in the barn. I guess I'll be takin' 'em, huh?" said Sam.

Bill shook his head. "I can take 'em."

Sam looked at his son. "I think you better give it a few more days, Bill. Four or five more baths in salts and I'll be able to sew it up. That's all I ask. You've come this far without complications. Give it another couple of days. I'll watch out for 'em."

Bill searched his father's eyes. It was a command, not a request, and Bill knew it. He cast a glance at Julie, then Mike, both of whom remained silent. They seemed to know it was a command too. Bill smiled. "Okay, Dad.

'Father knows best' is what I hear."

Sam sighed and smiled. "Don't worry about Mike and Julie. You'll be sewed up tight in a couple of days and livin' in that old cabin and wishing you were here to eat some of your mom's biscuits and gravy, and chili and beans."

Bill smiled weakly and leaned against the back of the sofa. "Yeah, you're right." He looked up at Mike. "Take the Uzi with you, Mike."

"Sure, Bill."

"Julie, take the Walther."

She nodded, her lower lip quivering. "What if they come here looking for us? What will you do?"

"Julie, this guy is a bondsman. He's not looking for me. I'll be all right. You just be sure and take everything you need in the way of clothes and supplies to last a couple of weeks with minimal resupply."

Julie stomped her foot. "Damn you, Bounty Hunter, there you go, barking orders again, like some damn drill sergeant. I know what to do." She turned and walked out of the room hurriedly.

Bill looked at Mike. "Did I say something wrong?"

Mike hunched up his shoulders. "I've never been able to figure her out. She's different, even for a woman."

"Men are so stupid." Frona strode after Julie.

The three men exchanged questioning looks.

"You suppose the rain's gonna ruin the cotton crop?" said Bill.

"Don't think so, but it might get too wet to plow," answered Sam.

Mike laughed as Bill and Sam smiled at one another.

CHAPTER 14

"Mornin', Ma." Bill brushed the curtain to the side of the kitchen window and gazed at the small mountains south of the house. "It sure is a pretty one."

"They've all been pretty since you started feeling better. Sit down at the table. Dad'll be here in a minute. It'll be good to see both of you at the table at the same time."

Bill pulled out a chair and sat carelessly as Sam walked into the kitchen. "Mornin', Dad."

"You look pretty chipper this morning."

Frona poured hot coffee into two large mugs and placed them in front of the men.

"Feel it too. How are Mike and Julie doin'?"

"Pretty good. Julie wants to take a bath, but I think Mike is havin' a good time under the circumstances. I think that Julie is sweet on you."

Bill felt the heat rise to his face. "Aw, Dad, it's just puppy love."

Frona put a plate of beans, beef and eggs roughly on the table. "I been meaning to talk to you about that girl, Bill. What are you going to do about her?"

"Do about her? What's to do? I'm going to take her and Mike to LA and that's the end of it. What are you talking about, Ma?"

"You know good 'n' well what I'm talking about. That girl's crazy over you, and you know it."

"She's not my type, Ma. And she's too young. For crying out loud, what's got into you? You don't even know her."

"I know her enough to know a thoroughbred when I see one. That young lady has class. She does her best to hide it -- I guess that's the thing to do these days -- but it shows through. She's a good girl, son."

"And she's not all that bad to look at," said Sam.

Frona slapped Sam on the arm with the spatula she held in her hand. "That'll be enough out of you, Sam Rutledge." She turned back to Bill, who looked intensely at his plate as he mopped up some beans with a flour tortilla. "I know it's none of my business, but I think you should give this girl a chance."

Bill looked up from his plate and smiled. "You know, that's the first time I ever heard you give me advice about my love life, and you sure picked a strange gal to start with. She's wanted for murder, Ma, or did you forget that little detail?"

"That girl didn't murder anybody, and neither did Mike, and we all know it."

"Well, anyway, I'm interested in Tom's sister -- not that it's any of your business." He winked.

"I don't know about her. Wasn't around her long enough to make a judgement. She seemed all right. But I'm telling you, that gal, Julie, is a pistol. She loves the ranch, and there's not a pretentious bone in her body. Dad and I are getting older and we're gonna have to retire in a few years. It would be nice if you and Julie could take over the place and make a go of it."

Bill held his mouth in mid-chew for a few seconds. He glanced at his father, who busily drank his coffee. "You've already got us married and living on the ranch? Are you in on this, Dad?" he said around the food in his mouth.

Sam put his cup on the table and shrugged. "I don't have anything to do with this. It would be nice if you moved onto the place and took things over in a few years, but it's getting harder and harder for a man to make it with a small spread. As far as Julie goes, it's like your mom says, I think she's a fine gal, but since I ain't the one who'd be marryin' her, it ain't for me to say. Tom's sister seemed might nice too. Hell, neither of us have seen one of your girlfriends at this house for years, and all of the sudden, we get two winners at a time." He grinned. "I don't know how you do it. I guess maybe that city life hasn't been all that bad for you after all."

Frona slapped him on the shoulder with the spatula again. "Sam, I'm bein' serious, and there you go joking about it."

"Who's joking?" He smiled up at her, the spatula waving menacingly near his nose.

"Well, it doesn't matter," said Bill. "I've got my sights set on Laura right now, if I ever get the time to chase her." He looked up at his mother. "Not that it's any of your business." His lips curled into a grin to match his father's.

"Eat your breakfast."

Bill knew his mother was through with the subject for now, but he also knew she would bring it up again. When she got something in her head, it was there to stay.

Bill finished the last of his breakfast, pushed the

plate away and looked at his father. "I'm ready for the stitches."

Sam shook his head. "I think we better give it a couple more days."

"I can't, Dad. I'm tired of those baths twice a day, and there's no infection. It's healed close enough to the surface. I'm ready."

Sam pushed his chair from the table. "Okay. I'll get my stuff. You just sit where you are. We can do it right here."

Frona looked at him nervously as Sam left the room. "Dad's pretty concerned about that wound. I mean, he's proud that it's healin' so well, but he's afraid something might go wrong and you'll get an infection."

"You kept it clean as a whistle that first week or so. If I didn't care about the size of the scar, you could have sewed me up in two weeks."

"I only cleaned it once. Julie watched me do it and she did it every time after that. Poor thing. She gagged every time she did it."

"I didn't know that."

"Yeah, I didn't figure she'd tell you. I'm tellin' ya, you're missin' the boat with that gal."

"Okay, Ma. Let it go for a minute, what do you say?" His thoughts drifted to the night he had found Julie in Mexico, then proceeded forward in time. He tried to sense the changes in her as they had made their escape. He couldn't pinpoint anything in particular, but there had been a change -- or had there? Maybe he had changed.

Sam walked into the kitchen, the brown leather bag in his hand. "You ready?"

Bill nodded. "You got pain killer?"

Sam turned to Frona. "Hon, get the whiskey bottle out, will you?"

"Whiskey bottle?" Bill sat up straight in the chair. "What's this about a whiskey bottle? What happened to good old fashioned Novocaine?"

"None left. I used what I had on you. That stuff is hard to come by these days."

"Oh jeez, I didn't really need to hear that." He faced his mother. "Ma, get that bottle of whiskey over here, quick."

She placed a bottle of Jack Daniels on the table and sat across from him. "Normally, we only use it for snake bite, but I'll make an exception in your case." She gave him a wink.

Bill took off his shirt and pulled the bottle of whiskey to his empty coffee cup. He poured three fingers into the cup and downed it in a swallow, smacking his lips as he set the cup back on the table. He shook his head and made a face. "It's too early in the morning for that stuff. Whew!"

"Hold still," said Sam as he slapped the skin around the wound briskly with his fingers.

"Ow. What are you doing, trying to give me a 'pinky'?"

"Yep. Tell me when it hurts like hell and you can't stand it anymore. The longer you can stand it, the less you'll feel the needle."

Bill gritted his teeth and held his breath as the heat in his skin near the wound rose to an almost unbearable level. "That's it! Whoa."

Quickly, Sam stopped slapping the skin and picked up his prepared suture needle. "This won't be too bad."

He looked over his shoulder. "You wanna help hang onto him, just in case he decides to wimp out on us?"

Frona moved to his side.

"Thanks, that's all I needed," mumbled Bill as the needle made its first pass. He gritted his teeth and smiled up at Sam. "Nothin' personal, but your bedside manner leaves a little bit to be desired." He clamped his jaw tightly as the needle scored again.

Sam smiled. "You're not doin' too bad for a city slicker."

"City slicker?" Bill shook his head. "Later, Dad. Later." He gulped in as much air as he could take in one deep breath and held it.

Sam worked quickly and confidently. In a few minutes, he was finished. He stepped back and surveyed his work with a broad smile. "I think I should have been a doctor."

"A horse doctor maybe," said Bill as he drew in another breath.

The songs of several crickets lulled Bill into a false sense of security as he sat on the front porch of his parents' house. He momentarily forgot the recent turn of events in his life and how the length of his future was more than questionable. The night sounds of the Sonoran Desert brought back memories of his youth and the adventures of a young boy with his own horse and dog, and of the trails they had traveled together. He stared into the dark shadows cast by a large mesquite in the silver light of a half moon and was jolted out of his reverie.

Sam, who sat in the rocker next to him, said, "What is it? You hear something?"

Bill shook his head. "No but a thought occurred to me. Do you still have my old single-action Colt and holster around here somewhere?"

"It's hangin' on a peg in your old closet. Never had any need to move it."

The rocker creaked as Bill stood. "I think I'd like to clean it up and carry it. I used to be pretty fast with that thing when I was a kid."

Sam stood. "That's a damned understatement. Hell, I know you told me there were guys faster than you but I never believed it."

"It's true, Dad. Not *much* faster, but they *were* faster. Not many were faster and as accurate though," said Bill with more than an ounce of pride as he stepped into his old room and turned on the light.

"You're not planning on doin' any of that quick-draw stuff yet are you? Hell, we just sewed you up today."

"I'll start slow, Dad. Don't worry. I'm not going to mess up all of your good work just to practice." He opened the closet door. From the peg at eye-level on the left end of the closet he lifted the buscadero holster and single-action Colt and brought it into the light of the room.

He removed the pistol from the holster, opened the loading gate and checked to see if it was unloaded. It wasn't. He emptied the six rounds of .357 magnum ammo onto the small desk on the side of the room to the left of his bed. The pistol had light surface rust on the barrel and a little around the trigger guard but it was nothing serious. *Thank God for the dry air around here*, he thought.

Sam said, "I haven't cleaned it for a couple of years but it's just the way you left it. Sorry about that little bit of rust. I was gonna get to it later in the year."

Bill smiled. "Thanks for takin' care of it, Dad. I haven't had much use for it this past twenty-five years. I almost forgot about it completely."

"Your ma and I never forgot about it. We still have your trophies you won at them contests. Every one of 'em. Hell, Ma and me had more fun at them shindigs than most of the contestants. Except that one they held up in Phoenix. Too many city-slickers. We've got a bunch of pictures in the album if you want to take a look at them someday."

Bill smiled, his mind recalling those days of youth and glory. "Maybe someday I will. Right now, I don't want to be reminded of the age difference between me and the kid in those pictures."

Sam reached into the closet and withdrew a cleaning kit from a corner of the floor. "Here. It's all there except a few patches."

Bill spread a cloth from the kit on the top of the desk and removed the cylinder from the pistol. He checked the bore and found it in pretty good shape, considering the number of rounds, both blank and ball, that had been fired through it. He began the cleaning process.

Sam sat on the bed and pulled out a sack of Bull Durham. After he had rolled one, pulled the sack string tight with his teeth and put the makings back in his shirt pocket, he said, "I've seen you in a bunch of scrapes over the years, but don't you think you might've outdone yourself a bit with this one?"

Bill looked up from the solvent-covered cylinder in his hand. "That's puttin' it on the mild side, Dad. It all happened so fast and, once it got started, there was no stoppin' it."

"It ain't gonna end with you turnin' them two in, is it?"

Bill shook his head. "I don't really suspect it will. There's a bunch of mad Mexicans that aren't going to let it go. I'm not so worried about the Federales as I am the real bad guys. I think I may have made 'em a little madder than what they're willing to write off."

"From what I hear, you did 'em more damage than Pershing did in 1916."

"You been listening to Mike and Julie too much. I only did what I had to do to get us out of there." Bill turned his attention back to the pistol.

"What are your plans, if you don't mind me asking?"

Bill looked up from the cylinder and cocked his head to one side, staring at the wall opposite. "I don't really know. Maybe I'll disappear into Montana or something."

Sam shook his head. "I know better. It's too damn cold up there for you."

Bill smiled, wiped the cylinder with a light coat of oil, placed it on the oilcloth, and began work on the rest of the pistol. "Yeah. I guess you're right there. I'll figure something out when the time comes."

"What are you gonna do about Julie?"

"Not you too, Dad."

"Well, that gal kinda grows on ya'."

"Yeah, So does cancer. I wasn't shot at as many times in Viet Nam as I've been since I met her. I'm gettin' tired of it."

Sam grinned. "I thought you liked a little excitement

in your life?"

"A little? I believe I've had about all the excitement I want for next hundred or so years."

Sam stubbed out his cigarette in the porcelain ashtray on the desk. "Well, I guess I'm gonna hit the hay. Ma is probably wondering where I got off to."

"Night, Dad. And thanks."

"Night."

When he was satisfied his work was done, Bill assembled the weapon and put it into the holster, then picked it up and strapped it on. It felt good.

CHAPTER 15

Bill stood, legs apart the width of his shoulders, hunched over, left hand an inch from the pistol on his hip. He focused his attention on the paper plate he had placed against the bank of the wash. In the blink of an eye, he drew the Colt, thumbed the hammer back and pulled the trigger. The pistol recoiled from the fired round's energy. Bill holstered it and squinted at the plate, fifteen yards in front of him. There was a .357 caliber hole an inch from center at one o'clock. *Not bad for an old man*, he thought. He was pleased with his ability. He had been concerned that he would need to practice for hours before he recaptured his skill with a single-action revolver, but he had only been at it five minutes and that had been the first round he had fired.

Maybe he wasn't quite as fast as he used to be but he was still as accurate. That was what counted for him. He figured his speed would improve with the healing of the wound. He didn't delude himself into thinking that a single-action Colt was the answer to all of his problems but it was good enough to answer a few of them.

His chest felt a little tight in the area of the stitches and he decided to pack it in for the day and return to the house. No sense pushing things too far. He picked up the plate and turned to see his father, sitting his bay, up on the shallow bank on the opposite side of the wash. Rufus, the cow dog, sat nearby on the shade of a mesquite.

"Not bad shootin'. I never could figure out how you did that. Hell, I tried it once, when you were in your heyday, and damn near blew off my foot."

Bill walked across the wash toward him. "That could happen to anybody. I've almost done it myself a time or two."

"Then maybe you should stick to a rifle."

"A great idea, but not very practical."

"Ma sent me down here to get you. Lunch is ready."

"I'm on the way."

Sam sat the saddle slouched while Bill climbed the bank and untied his roan, which was tethered to a mesquite, stuffed the paper plate into a saddlebag, mounted and rode slowly toward the house, his mind wandering but his eyes taking in all that could be seen. Rufus trotted in and out of the creosote and mesquite on the right flank. That dog loved to explore. The only thing he enjoyed more was working cattle.

After a few moments Sam said, "Thought I saw someone on foot down by the San Pedro this mornin', about a half mile south of the split cottonwood."

"Get a good look?" asked Bill.

"Naw, hell. I was lookin' for that ol' brindle steer and had just found 'im when I caught a glimpse. Didn't give it much thought until about ten minutes later. I rode back to the spot where I thought I saw him but nobody was there."

"Maybe it was just a coyote."

"Could be but I don't think so, unless he was wearin' size eleven dress shoes."

"Dress shoes? For walkin' around in the desert?" Bill reined up. Sam stopped next to him.

Sam shrugged. "We've both seen worse than that.

You remember when you were a kid and we found those tourist out in the middle of the desert in June, wearing shorts, no hats and packin' no water? They pert near died. Some people are just ignorant. We all gotta learn someway."

Bill squinted west, toward the San Pedro, which was out of sight, but he could see the line of cottonwoods on its banks. "I think I'll take a quick look."

"Ma ain't gonna like this. You reckon it could wait till after lunch?"

Bill smiled. "I better not. It might just be a lost tourist but I really can't take the chance. That bondsman in L.A. would do about anything to snatch Julie and Mike from me." He nudged his roan gently in the flanks.

"When you gonna ride out to the shack?" asked Sam as he drew alongside.

"I figured I'd go out and see them tomorrow. How they doin'?"

"They seem to be doin' fine but I know Julie would rather be at the house."

"Who wouldn't? Running water and Ma's cookin'," said Bill.

A smile spread across Sam's face. "Those are good reasons, I'll grant you, but I think her main reason is a fella named Bill."

"She hasn't forgot about me yet?"

"Not likely. The first words out of her mouth every time I've dropped in on 'em have been, 'How's Bill?.'"

"She'll grow out of it," said Bill unconvincingly.

"Maybe." Sam paused. "But I wouldn't be too sure of that if I were you."

"She's not going to have a choice in the matter. I'm

tired of talkin' about it. You mind if we change the subject?"

Sam laughed. "You think the Yankees are gonna win the pennant?"

It was a line they used between them when they wanted to change the direction of a conversation. Bill joined in the laughter."I suspect they have a damn good chance of doin' just that."

"Off to the right, about a hundred yards." Sam gestured.

The bank of the San Pedro River was high at this point but the water was low and Bill spotted the footprints from quite some distance away. He followed them across the sand to the west bank and dismounted, tethering his roan to a bush. Sam remained mounted next to him. He rarely left the saddle unless it was an absolute requirement.

Bill said, "You might want to pull that Winchester and keep a watch from here. I'm gonna take a quick look to the west."

Sam nodded and pulled his Model 94 lever-action 30-30 from the saddle holster.

With a short glance over his shoulder, Bill climbed the bank and followed the tracks made by the dress shoes. There was a dirt trail, occasionally used by four-wheel drive vehicles, about a half-mile west of the river and he suspected the tracks would end there. He used caution in his approach to the trail but it was unnecessary. There had been a vehicle and it was gone. The curious thing was, another set of footprints led to the vehicle from the south. Two men, each going in a different direction. Certainly not common for tourists, and there were no hunters out this time of year.

The vehicle had made a turnaround and headed north, toward Interstate 10. He looked for a dust cloud in that direction but saw nothing. They were most likely long gone. He returned to the river.

Sam was afoot, next to his bay, sitting in the shade of a cottonwood, smoking a roll-your-own.

"I thought you were gonna keep watch," said Bill.

"I was but there wasn't much sense in that once you dropped out of sight. I was better off hidden. Besides, my horse didn't like standing out there in the sun."

"Oh. I see. The horse didn't like it. That kinda says it all, don't it?"

Bill unsaddled the roan and turned it loose in the corral south of the house. He watched his father take off his spurs on the front porch and kick the dirt from his boots before entering the living room and smiled at the simplicity of a ritual that he had observed off and on for the better part of forty years. It really is the little things in life that make it worth living, he thought, as he climbed between the rails in the corral fence.

The tracks near the San Pedro bothered him but not enough to miss one of his mother's lunches. The tracks were obviously made by city men and, though they may be the best old Bernie had, they weren't good enough to take Mike and Julie from this place. He smelled the chili and fresh beef through the screen door and his stomach growled insistently.

"Smells good, Ma," he said as he walked by the kitchen on his way to the sink to wash his hands.

"A little bit longer and Rufus would'a' got it. What

took you two so long?"

"Dad spotted the tracks of a pair of city-slickers and we followed them a ways. I think the bondsman from L.A. has a few men out looking for Mike and Julie. I'm gonna take a ride to the old line shack tomorrow and check on 'em."

Frona nodded. "They're about due for some supplies. I've got them in the pantry." She spooned fresh pinto beans and red chili onto plates then placed them on the table next to a large platter of tortillas. "Cooked your favorite. Had a feelin' you wouldn't be around for supper -- so you can have it for lunch."

"Thanks, Ma." He sat and scooted his chair to the table.

"You gonna wear that pistol at the table?"

"I think I better, Ma. I don't want caught without a weapon if things get bad."

Frona looked at him intently for a moment. "In all the years you've been doing this silly business, I've never seen you wear a gun to the table."

"In all the years I've been doing it, I never saw a need before. I'm sorry I brought this on you and dad. I wasn't in any condition to look for other options."

Sam joined them and waited patiently for Frona to be seated. They ate in silence and Bill was grateful for it. He mulled over the tracks and the presence of the two men and wondered how they planned to take Mike and Julie from him. It wasn't something that was done every day. Stealing a bail jumper from a bounty hunter could become a dicey proposition. He was curious as to how much Bernie was paying them.

He rolled a tortilla and soaked up the last of the

chili. "This is great, Ma. Thanks."

"I'm glad you like it."

After several moments of silence, his mother said, "What's botherin' you?"

"Who said anything was botherin' me?" said Bill defensively.

"I did. Now, what is it?"

Sam looked from his wife to his son then took in a mouthful of beans.

Bill said, "It's the tracks." He paused for a moment. "I think I'd better ride out tonight. I don't think those city boys will be into sittin' out in the desert all night."

Sam said, "Take Rufus. He needs the exercise."

Bill knew that to be a lie. Rufus never needed exercise. That dog was a bundle of inexhaustible energy, but he did love to flank a horse and, if you carried a rifle, he was sure he was going hunting. That was another one of those things Rufus dearly loved. "Yeah, that's not a bad idea."

Shortly after three in the morning, Bill saddled up and rode from the ranch house, Rufus appearing a bit confused about the hour but eagerly flanking the roan on the right as they left the ranch house. Bill had left the Colt in his room at the house. He didn't feel the need to carry the extra weight. The M-1 Garand in the saddle scabbard would be more than enough protection. He glanced over his shoulder and caught the feint red glow of a cigarette in his parents' bedroom window. His father would never admit it but he was concerned. He wasn't a man to lose sleep without cause, nor was he a man to get up and smoke a cigarette at three in the morning.

Bill was in no hurry. He didn't want to arrive before daylight. If he dawdled long enough, he would arrive at the line cabin about that time. His purpose in leaving the house during the hours of darkness was to evade prying eyes, not to sneak up on Mike and Julie. About two miles from the ranch house he rode through a dry wash and paused to enjoy the night air in the moon shadow of a large mesquite.

He wondered what Laura was doing and if he would be rid of Mike and Julie in time to find out before she found a significant other. He visualized the late afternoon sun bouncing from her auburn hair as they drove into Guaymas. That should have been enough to make him quit this business right then and there.

He unconsciously reached for his shirt pocket then drew his hand away empty. This was no time for a smoke. Laura didn't smoke, as far as he knew. He might have to think about quitting. His thoughts drifted to Julie for a moment. She wouldn't care one way or the other if he smoked. He shook his head to rid himself of the thought and nudged the roan forward. The big gelding moved quickly, eager to be on the move again. Bill had to rein him in a bit.

The grey dawn was giving up its first glimpse of the day when he reined in at the top of the small hill overlooking the cabin. He sat the roan silently for a few minutes and searched the surrounding area with his eyes. Nothing seemed out of the ordinary. Still he waited.

One of the two horses in the small corral snorted loudly and Mike stepped outside. Bill smiled as he watched Mike pick up a chunk of hay from the end of a bale near the west side of the cabin and carry it to the corral. Mike said something to the horses as he tossed the hay into the corral. Bill couldn't hear what was said but he didn't figure it to be much in the way of praise. The horses whinnied softly and proceeded to the hay and breakfast.

As Mike turned from the corral and faced in Bill's direction, he spotted the rider, sitting his horse silently on the small hill. For an instant, it appeared that Mike was going to run for the house and a weapon.

"It's me, Mike, your worst nightmare," shouted Bill around a broad smile as he urged his mount down the hill.

Mike's lips curved upward in a grin as he stepped forward to meet him. "I'll be damned! I thought we got rid of you for good."

Bill reined up next to him and said, "I guess your run of bad luck is still with you."

"Did you bring any supplies?" asked Mike.

Bill jerked his head to the saddle pack behind him. "The latest issue of House and Garden and a little grub."

Mike frowned and removed the saddle pack. "Julie's cookin' breakfast. We better tell her you're here so she can throw on some more beans."

About then, Julie stepped out of the cabin and rushed to meet him. Bill tightened his pull on the reins to keep the roan from bolting. Julie slowed as she neared and composed herself about the time Bill had the roan under control.

"Hi, Bounty Hunter!" she said as she stepped near the horse.

Bill dismounted and she hugged him quickly but gently. He shook Mike's hand and led the horse to the corral where Mike unsaddled him and turned him loose inside. As he closed the corral gate, Mike said, "You look pretty good for a guy who was on his deathbed a short while ago."

"I'm doin' all right. How are you two makin' out?"

"Never felt better. I never knew life could be so peaceful. I'm thinkin' about askin' your dad if he needs another hand on this place," smiled Mike.

"Me too," said Julie. "Why did you ever leave this place?"

He smiled at her. "These small ranches aren't going to be around much longer. Thought I'd get into a more modern line of work."

She cocked her head, "Oh, you mean something as modern as bounty hunting?"

"Somebody's gotta do it."

Mike said, "Let's eat." He started for the cabin.

Julie said, "Damn!" and bolted for the cabin.

Bill stepped inside to the smell of burning bacon and a dense wall of smoke.

"Damn! Damn! Damn!" Julie said as she place a rag around her hand, lifted the heavy cast iron skillet from the stove and carried it outside. She returned in a moment with the empty frying pan. "I hope Rufus likes burnt bacon."

"He likes any kind of bacon," said Bill, smiling broadly.

"Well, he's getting the bacon and all you two get is beans and bread."

"My favorite," said Bill, still smiling. "I did bring some eggs."

"Eggs?" said Mike as he rummaged through the saddle pack.

Mike cooked toast in a skillet while Julie scrambled eggs. The eggs were supposed to be fried but when two of them broke upon impact with the frying pan, Julie quickly decided that scrambled would be a better way to go.

During the morning meal, no one spoke. Julie looked at him constantly and made no effort to hide that fact. When they were finished, Bill said, "I'm pretty sure a couple of the bondsman's boys have found out about the ranch. It's probably only a matter of time until they find this cabin."

"What does that mean for us?" asked Julie.

"I don't know yet. I'm trying to work out a plan but nothing definite has come up yet."

"Great," said Mike.

"I didn't want us to have to move just yet but it may come to that. In the meantime, you two had best keep a close eye out. I'm gonna get back to the ranch and see what I can do to beef up security."

Mike looked worried. Julie looked more sad than worried.

"I like this place, Bounty Hunter."

Bill nodded. "Me too, kid. Me too." He stood and walked to the corral.

The sound of a car approaching the house at a high rate of speed drew Bill out of the chair. He rushed to the fireplace, grabbed a Winchester from above the mantle and headed for the porch.

A late model Plymouth slid to a stop at the step. The door opened and Laura emerged from a cloud of dust to rush up to the porch where Bill and his parents stood.

"Oh, God! I'm so glad you're all right -- all of you."

"What are you talking about? Is something wrong?" asked Bill.

"Come inside, Laura. Have a sit and a cup of coffee and tell us all about it," said Frona.

Laura seemed frantic. Her eyes went to the sutures on Bill's chest. He eased the Winchester to the planks, butt first. "Yeah, come on inside and tell us what this is all about. You look nice this morning."

"This is important, Bill. Hear me out. Then maybe you won't want me to have coffee in your house -- any of you."

"This girl is upset." Frona put her arm around Laura's shoulders and led her through the door and into the kitchen.

Laura's hands trembled as she held the cup between them. She looked up at Bill as he returned from putting the Winchester in its proper place. "Bill, I work for the newspaper."

"So? I can overlook that." He smiled, but he felt something he didn't want to hear was about to be said.

"I write a column -- under the name of Ruth Borden."

"Oh, yeah, I've read it once or twice. Sorry I haven't had time to get a Tucson paper recently. I'll make up for it in a little while though."

Tears began to run down her cheeks. "I'm so sorry, Bill."

"Sorry? For what -- working for the newspaper?"

Frona pinched his arm gently. "Let her talk in her own time."

"I was doing a series on guns and violence in

Tucson when Tom took me to your place. He said you were a good subject to talk to, but that was supposed to come later, after we got to know each other." She looked up into his eyes. "I was going to tell you before I printed a thing, Bill, I swear it."

"What are you driving at, Laura?"

Again he felt his mother's fingers pinch his arm.

"After that night in Guaymas when all that shooting took place, and we didn't hear from you, Tom and I both thought you were dead, or in a Mexican prison." She took a sip of her coffee. "I printed the story -- what I knew of it -- of the gunfight in the bar."

Bill felt a pounding in his temples. "You didn't use my name, did you?" He held his breath and waited for her answer.

"I told about how the other men shot first, at someone else in the bar, and how you pushed me to the floor and shot at the men with the guns --"

"Laura! Did you mention my name?"

She nodded, biting her quivering lower lip until it was almost bleeding.

"Jesus!" Bill looked at his father. "I don't know why you haven't been contacted yet, but eventually they'll find this place. You and Ma gotta get out of here."

"We're not going anywhere. We've got animals to tend and work to be done. I'm not gonna let a bunch of wetbacks run us from our own place," said Frona vehemently.

"Ma, there's no time to argue. These aren't your ordinary, everyday wetbacks. These people are cold-blooded killers. Grab some things and go to Safford for a few days. I'll get Mike and Julie and head for LA. I'll make it known in the right circles that we aren't here and then I'll call you at Uncle Jack's when I know the coast is clear."

"I'm sorry, Bill," repeated Laura.

"When did you run the story?"

"The day before you called Tom."

"What took you so long to tell us?"

"I didn't realize until this morning that some of those people might read the story and put it all together. I don't know how many people know about your parents." She looked up at Frona. "I'm so sorry."

Frona patted her on the shoulder. "Don't worry about it. It's done and over with." She looked at her son. "We were just in Safford last month. I think I'll stay home."

"Ma, you can't."

"Oh? And who says so?"

Sam said, "You might want to think it over, Hon. Things will be all right for a couple of days."

She looked at Sam. "I'm not going anywhere. I'll be damned if I'm gonna let a bunch of Mexicans run me from my own land. They did it to my grandfather with a little fat man with a bushy mustache, and I'll be damned if they're gonna do it to me."

"These people have machine guns, Ma. Winchesters won't stop 'em."

"That little bastard Poncho Villa had machine guns too."

Bill knew it was useless to argue with her. The stories of Poncho Villa's raids into Arizona and New Mexico were part of his family history. She would never run from an invading Mexican army -- not even if it crossed into Arizona with tanks and artillery.

"I'll get Julie and Mike. You should go into Benson and let the sheriff know what's going on. Maybe he could send out some extra help, but I don't have much confidence in that. They don't have the manpower to cover their routine jobs." He looked into his mother's eyes. "And, Ma, I'm tellin' ya, one deputy isn't enough. These people travel in packs -- just like wolves -- and they've got less conscience."

Sam raised an eyebrow. "You know, the more I think about this, the madder I get. We'll take care of ourselves."

"You gotta sleep, Dad."

"Please. This is crazy," said Laura.

All eyes turned to her.

"I've caused all of this. You can stay at my place."

"They'll get to you eventually too, Laura. If they can't find me here, they'll be at your front door some night."

"What can we do?" she asked.

"I guess the only thing to do is to turn Julie and Mike in a little early and hope they forget about me and my family."

"That plan is full of holes, son," said Frona. "You whipped them Mexicans at their own game and they aren't going to forget it, even if you turn in Julie and Mike. That'll probably make things worse. I don't see an end to it."

Bill considered her words as he stared out the kitchen window. She was right. The only thing that would ensure his parents' safety would be for him to turn Julie and Mike and himself over to the Mexicans. He swallowed hard as he imagined how they would die. He remembered the DEA agent who had been brutally tortured and killed only a few years ago by this same group. He felt fear and frustration flow through his body.

Sam smiled. "Hell, we could invade Mexico -- take 'em in their own backyard by surprise. A few of the boys around here would go along with us, I'm sure."

Bill shook his head. "There's no easy way out -- that's for sure -- but that's stretching it, Dad." He paused. "Would you saddle a horse for me? I'll go after Julie and Mike. We can be out of here in the morning. Meantime, Laura should go to town and tell the sheriff what's going on. You and mom keep the Winchesters ready and a sharp lookout." He looked at Laura. "Can you wait in Benson for us? If Dad can get us there, I'd appreciate a ride to Tucson. Meet us at the train stop. There's nothing there but a sign and a bench."

Laura nodded. "I'm sorry, Bill. I didn't realize what was going on."

"It's done now, Laura. Don't worry about it. What's to do is to square things away."

Sam stepped out of the house and headed for the coral, mumbling about an invasion of Mexico sounding like a good idea to him.

In five minutes, Bill was in the saddle, his M-1 stuffed into Sam's Winchester rifle boot, a canteen of water slung carelessly over the saddle horn. He felt like he had just stepped back in time with the single-action colt strapped to his left thigh in a buscadero holster. It was a relic of his younger days when he had been involved in a quick-draw club. He looked down at his parents, standing next to the horse. "Seems like I saw this scene in a John Wayne movie once. I sure hope it turns out the same way. The only thing I'm missing is the hat."

"I'll get the sheriff to come out right away."

He smiled down at the beauty that was Laura. "Don't forget the second part."

She nodded. "I'll be at the train stop."

"Dad, Ma, be careful. I should be back before daylight. Once I get them into Tucson, I'll make a few calls and throw 'em off this place."

"Don't you worry about us, son. Me and your dad can take care of ourselves. We been doin' it long enough to know how."

Bill smiled and clucked to his horse.

CHAPTER 16

Bill thought about the West as it must have been more than a hundred years before his time. The horse and the single-action Colt made him feel that way -- like someone from long ago, drifting to wherever his horse or his desires took him, with no burden of responsibility for anything or anyone other than himself.

He looked across the vast expanse of low mountains and desert and saw where the grasslands took over the landscape only a few miles to the south. Rufus ran parallel to him, on his right, searching for rabbits. *That dog loves to hunt. He's going to be awfully disappointed when he shakes something up and I don't shoot it.*

The old, line cabin was in the first range of hills, just south of the grass line and about four miles into the mountains. He stopped and let his horse blow on a small ridge, looking behind him, wondering whatever happened to Bernie's men. He had deliberately taken a route impassible by vehicle, even the best of the four-wheel-drives, but there was always the chance that they had horses. It wasn't likely, but he had to be careful.

All pain had long since left his chest, and except for the stitches, he felt nothing unusual physically. He lifted the canteen to his lips and drank sparingly, then wet his hand and reached over the saddle horn and let the horse have a taste of the cool water. Rufus panted at the horse's side. Bill stepped out of the saddle and poured some water into a cupped hand, which Rufus quickly lapped up. Bill remounted.

As he pushed onward, he thought of taking up a new way of life. Maybe he could be a teacher. Hell, he could even go back to school and get a degree in medicine -- be a doctor.

His mind came back to the present and his eyes darted across the horizon, fear that he had been careless flashed through his head. He saw nothing, but he felt something intangible, almost surreal. He couldn't shake it. He pointed his horse west, into the setting sun and rode for an hour, in the hopes he would shake the feeling tormenting him -- the feeling of being followed. He shook his head. *Bernie's men can't be that good. They're all city boys.*

It was shortly after sunset when he left the saddle and tied his horse to a pinion tree. He proceeded the last two hundred yards on foot, approaching the cabin from the high ground to the south. He knelt next to a scrub oak and watched the cabin below. Mike stepped outside and turned his head from side to side, then opened the door to the cabin and Julie joined him outside.

Bill felt like a peeping Tom as he watched Julie step from under the rickety mesquite awning over the front door. Somehow it just didn't seem right to watch her without her knowledge. Rufus sat next to him, eying him suspiciously. He stood and shouted. "Hello, the cabin. It's Bill."

Mike spun and fired the Uzi at the hills south of him, missing Bill by at least a hundred yards. The burst was short, and Mike released the trigger when he realized he was shooting at Bill, who remained standing, a great distance from where he had fired.

Bill walked down the hill, his M-1 over his shoulder, barrel in his right hand, a broad smile on his face, Rufus at his side. "You don't shoot so good, Mike," he said when he got close enough to be heard without shouting.

"I'm sorry, man. You scared the hell out of me."

"Bounty Hunter!" Julie rushed to greet him, throwing her arms around him and causing him to lower the rifle. Rufus wagged his tail in greeting.

"Whoa! Take it easy."

She kissed him on the cheek and backed away, appearing suddenly self-conscious.

"Christ, all you need is a cowboy hat to look like one of those bad guys in the western movies. What's with the old-fashioned pistol and holster?"

"It just looks old-fashioned. It's a single-action all right, but it's a .357 magnum. I used to use it years ago when I was into that quick draw kind of stuff."

"What haven't you been into, Bounty Hunter?" smiled Julie.

"Some other time, Julie. There's been a few things go kind of wrong, and I think we're in danger. So are my folks. We've got to change our plans."

"Your folks? What have they got to do with us?" There was concern in Mike's voice.

"They hid us, Mike, remember?"

"What kind of trouble? Are their lives in danger? You mean that kind of trouble?" asked Julie.

Bill nodded in the waning light. "Yeah, I mean that kind of trouble. And I'm not puttin' their lives in jeopardy --

not even for you two. We're headed for LA. C'mon, grab your gear and let's get going. I'll give the horses some of the hay you've got left and then we're leaving."

"LA? You got to be kidding?" Mike raised the barrel of the Uzi slightly, pointing in Bill's direction.

"Mike! Damnit, he said his parents were in danger," her voice was stern.

"Yeah, but, sis -- LA?"

"Put the Uzi down, Mike, or so help me, I'll kill you," said Bill.

"You'll kill me? Are you crazy?" Mike raised the barrel to bear on Bill's chest. "I've got you in my sights, man."

Rufus bared his teeth and uttered a quiet growl.

"Mike!" Julie's voice was almost a scream.

He lowered the Uzi and looked at his feet. "I'm sorry, man. I guess I'm just afraid of dying like a trapped rat."

"I didn't say I was going to turn you in just yet. I'll borrow some money and put us up somewhere until I have a little more time to come up with a better plan. Now get your gear and let's get moving."

Silently, they both stepped into the cabin while Bill fed the horses and saddled them. In ten minutes, with the sun well out of sight, they moved out of the hills and into the grasslands. After several minutes, Julie spoke. "Bounty Hunter, what are you really going to do with us?"

He felt a pang of guilt as he heard her words. His parents had to come first. "I've got to let those boys from Mexico know that we're not at my folk's place. The only way I know how to do that is to show up somewhere else and be identified. Now, if you can fill in the blanks without being turned in, I'm willing to listen."

He felt his back muscles stiffen at the thought of Mike pulling the trigger on that Uzi behind him. With Julie between them, he might be more reticent.

They rode in silence for another minute. "Don't you ever try to bullshit, just a little, Bounty Hunter? I mean, it wouldn't have hurt you to tell a little white lie and keep us happy, would it? Let us walk into this thing fat, dumb and happy? No, you've got to tell it like it is. You make a person feel like a piece of...nothing." Julie's voice cracked.

Bill reined in and waited for her horse to stop behind him. "Look, I don't want any of this. I'm tired of both of you. I don't think you killed anybody, but that doesn't mean I have to risk my parents' lives. When we get back to the house, I'm taking you to Benson. Laura will pick you up and get you to Tucson. From there, you're on your own. Just get out of my life, understand?"

"You mean you're letting us go?" asked Mike.

Bill sighed. "Mike, don't you understand what it means to be tired of something -- to just want to be rid of it?"

"Just like that?"

"Just like that. Now, can we get on with it? The sooner you two are out of my life, the better." He tapped his horse lightly in the flanks with his boots. The creak of saddle leather and the soft "clop" of hooves told him they were close behind.

A three-quarter moon lit up the eastern horizon as they left the grassland and moved through the desert. Rufus moved about on their flanks, a darting shadow in the moonlight.

"Bounty Hunter?"

"Yeah, Julie?"

"We've been through a lot together, you know that? Probably more than most people will ever go through together in a dozen lifetimes."

"Chalk it up to experience and go on to something better."

"What's better?" asked Mike.

"What's better? What kind of question is that?"

"Yeah, what's better? We just lived through a dozen Hollywood adventure movies, and we're still alive. We made it. It could be worse."

"It's not over yet, Mike."

"We'll come out of it winners. You'll just be short two-hundred-thousand dollars. I still can't believe you're going to do that."

Bill stared into the desert before him. "I personally don't care what you believe."

"But why? I don't get it," said Julie.

"Forget why. Who knows? I'm not even sure I know why. Don't look a gift horse in the mouth. Just pick up your marbles and get out of my life."

"I'm not forgetting why, Bounty Hunter. I want to know."

Bill turned in the saddle. "Look, you, I've got a name. Use it if you want to talk to me."

"Bounty Hunter suits you better than Bill. I've thought it over."

"Mike, tell her to shut up before I change my mind."

"Shut up, sis. Leave things well enough alone."

The rest of the ride to the ranch house was completed in silence. The kitchen light was on as they approached the house. Bill smiled to himself. That would be his mother -- like when he had been a kid -- she always waited up for him.

He unsaddled the horses and rubbed them briefly with hay while Mike and Julie went into the house with their gear. Rufus stood next to him as he turned the horses loose in the coral. He looked down at the old cow dog. "You know, Rufe, I can't figure it out. I think I'm more bothered by the thought of never seeing Julie again than I am about losing the two-hundred-thousand."

Rufus cocked his head to one side.

Bill closed the coral gate. "I don't understand it either, old boy. She just kind of grows on you, I guess -- you know -- like athlete's foot or something."

Rufus wagged his tail in apparent agreement and stepped out with Bill toward the house. At the door, Bill turned to Rufus. "You stay out here tonight and keep a lookout. We might have some company. If you see anything, let us know."

Rufus wagged his tail and moved to the end of the house as Bill opened the front door and stepped inside. "Is the coffee...?

His mother and father sat on the sofa near the fireplace, blood dripping from a cut in his father's forehead, his mother holding him around the shoulders. Mike was pinned to the floor, face down, an Uzi barrel pushed firmly behind his left ear, his arms spread wide on the carpet in front of the sofa. Julie sat next to his mother, a pistol pointed to her head. A third man stood behind the sofa, an Uzi held tightly, pointing at him.

Bill froze, the M-1 carried carelessly in his right hand, hanging below his waist.

"That's pretty smart for a gringo," said the man behind the sofa. "Now, why you don' drop the cannon gently to the floor, *amigo*?"

"What did you do to my father?"

"We talk when that cannon is on the floor, or we start shooting -- what you want?"

A fourth man stepped from the darkness of the small hallway. "Your father is all right, Mr. Rutledge. We just had to hit him over the head to calm him down."

"I'm sorry, son. They had your mom. I couldn't fight 'em. They would have killed her." Sam was near tears.

"They're going to anyway, Dad."

"The rifle, Mr. Rutledge," said the man in the hallway.

"Oh, my god! It's him -- Carrera -- in person," said Mike.

"For the last time, Mr. Rutledge -- put the rifle down."

Bill stared across the room at the infamous Carrera. He met the man's gaze head on and knew they were all dead. Gently, he placed the rifle on the carpet.

"Now the pistol, Mr. Rutledge. Unbuckle the belt."

Bill held his hand poised over the Colt. Carrera displayed no weapon -- that left three to contend with. He could get one, maybe two. By then, maybe Mike or his father could get to a gun. Time was running out. He knew once disarmed, they were all dead. If only he could even the odds a little. He had to do something fast. Death would wait but a few seconds more.

The living room window shattered as Rufus bounded into the room and went for the nearest man with a gun, the man who held Julie. Bill's hand dropped to his hip and came up full of casehardened steel. His first shot took the man behind the sofa in the center of the chest, slamming him into the wall. Bill fell to the floor to get an upward angle on his shot at the man pinning Mike, so that his bullet, if errant, wouldn't hit anyone on the sofa. The man was in the process of recovering from his surprise at the dog's entrance when Bill's second shot took him in the throat. His Uzi fired once into the floor and he fell over Mike.

Movement was everywhere in the room. Rufus clung to the gun arm of the man who had held Julie, the man swinging his arm as wildly as he could with an angry hundred-pound dog attached to it. Bill tried to get a shot, but was afraid of hitting the dog. He moved to his right for a better angle.

"No!" Julie screamed.

Bill rolled to his left as he heard the report of a semi-automatic pistol ring out several times. He turned, cocked the hammer back on his Colt, and fired at Carrera, who held his pistol pointed at him. Julie was on the floor. Carrera's head snapped back as the hundred-fifty-eight grain slug slammed into his skull at 1700 feet per second, the pistol in his hand falling harmlessly to the floor.

Bill turned his attention to the fourth man and Rufus. Mike and Sam had joined the fracas and had the man disarmed and pinned to the floor. Rufus stood over him, teeth bared in a vicious grin.

"Is everybody all right?"

"Oh, my god, Bill, Julie's been shot!" shouted Frona.

Bill turned to where he had seen her fall. She lay

on the floor in a pool of blood. Bill forgot where he was. He forgot who he was. He dropped his Colt and knelt next to her. There was a ringing in his ears that grew to a crescendo.

"No! Goddamnit! No!" He picked her up and carried her to the bedroom, placing her on the bed where he had only recently recuperated. "Ma! Get towels and bandages. Get me some hot water and soap." He didn't know if his mother had heard him or not. He looked into Julie's face. Her mouth was pulled tight in a grimace, her eyes straining to stay open. "Julie. Hang in there. You'll be all right." He pulled the sheath knife from his gunbelt and cut her blouse open, exposing two dark purple holes on her left side, just below her breast.

He looked away for a second to hide the fear he knew was on his face.

"I'm dying, aren't I, Bounty Hunter?"

He set his jaw and faced her. "Shut up, damnit! Save your strength. You're gonna make it -- you hear me?" He shouted over his shoulder. "Where are those towels?"

His mother rushed into the room. She placed the towels on the bed, turned on all the lights, and sat next to her son at Julie's side.

Bill wiped at the blood on her chest to better view the wounds. He almost whimpered as he fought to stop the flow of blood. "Ma, where's the water?"

"It's heating." She dabbed at one of the wounds. "You hang tough, Julie. I know you can do it, girl. You'll be all right."

Bill held his hands tightly over the wounds to stem the flow of blood. "Ma -- the water."

Mike passed her as she stepped out of the room. He knelt next to the bed and looked at his sister silently through tear-filled eyes.

"Where's the other Mexican?" asked Bill.

"Your dad has him tied up. Rufus is watching him." He nodded to Julie. "She's hurt bad, isn't she, man?"

"Yeah, she's hurt bad. Now why don't you shut up and make yourself useful or get the hell outa here."

"What do you want me to do?"

Get me some blankets and pillows, then get dad's pickup to the front door. Get some sleeping bags and make the bed as comfortable as you can."

Mike jumped to his feet and left the room.

Julie's eyes rolled back, leaving only the whites showing. Bill felt a panic deep inside. "Goddamnit, Peaches -- no!" He slapped her face gently.

"You'll kill her for sure that way, Bill. Let me at her. I'll bandage her up. You help get the truck ready."

Bill looked up at his mother. "No, Ma. I'm not leaving her."

"Well, then let's get her cleaned up and the bandages on."

They worked feverishly, Bill lifting Julie's torso while his mother applied the pressure bandages and tied them tight.

Mike shouted from outside. "The truck is ready!"

Bill leaned over the bed and picked Julie up gently. Carefully he carried her through the house and to the pickup idling near the front door. With Mike's help, he made her as comfortable as he could, propping her torso and head up with pillows, covering her with blankets, tucking them under her feet. Sam and Rufus escorted the

Mexican to the truck and sat him in the bed, Rufus at his side. Frona jumped into the front seat next to Sam and they moved quickly down the dirt road towards Benson, Sam using his knowledge of the road to miss as many of the bumps as possible.

Julie lay silently in the padded bed of the pickup, her breathing shallow and raspy, her eyes closed.

"I think one of her lungs has been hit," said Bill. He looked up at the Mexican, who sat with his back to the cab of the pickup. "If she dies, so do you, you son-of-a-bitch."

"I di'n't shoot her. I not know her."

Bill pushed blonde hair from Julie's eyes and looked back at the Mexican. "You know what? I personally don't give a damn. If she dies, you die -- only I'll see to it you suffer a long time before you're dead."

The whites of the Mexican's eyes glowed in the moonlight.

"How did you find us?"

The Mexican shrugged.

Bill hit him with a roundhouse left, slamming his head into the rear window of the truck. He then grabbed him by the front of his shirt and withdrew his sheath knife, holding it tightly against the man's testicles. "I asked you a question, asshole, and I want an answer -- now."

"A bondsman. Some bondsman in LA. Señor Carrera pay him two-hundred-thousand dollars. The bondsman say he only want his money back."

Bill's blood turned cold. He released his grip on the man and backed away until he was again next to Julie.

"The bondsman? The fucking bondsman?" said Mike.

"That low-life..."

Julie coughed and whimpered. Bill put his head next to her mouth and listened to her breathing. He lay next to her and brushed her hair from her face. "Hang in there, Peaches. We'll be in Benson in a few minutes."

Sam parked the truck at the train stop and Bill jumped out. "Get her to the hospital."

"Aren't you coming?" asked Frona.

Bill shook his head. "There's nothing I can do for her now. I've got some business to take care of. Give the sheriff all the details. I'll be back." He waved and ran to Laura's Plymouth, sitting on the other side of the tracks.

Her doors were locked and she was fast asleep when he approached, but she awoke with a start when he tapped the window. She opened her door and stepped into the night. "Are you okay? Where's Mike and Julie?"

"They're on their way to the hospital here in Benson. Julie's been shot pretty bad."

She put her hand to her mouth.

"C'mon, we've got to get to Tucson."

"What about Mike and Julie?"

"They'll have to wait. I've got business to take care of in LA."

CHAPTER 17

It was almost noon when Bill stepped into the air-conditioned atmosphere of Los Angeles International Airport, his credit card another ninety dollars heavier. He hailed a cab and gave the driver the address to AAAA Bail Bonds.

The plane trip to LA had given him too much time to think about the future. He had come to LA to kill Bernie. He knew Julie would die, of that there was little doubt. He wondered if she had even made it to the hospital. For that, Bernie had to die.

But why? Why was he thinking like a vengeful killer, when he considered himself a civilized man? His life would be worth nothing if he killed Bernie. He would spend the rest of his days in a California prison. There would be no tinkering with his muscle cars, or evenings with Laura, or even the sounds and smells of the desert he loved so much.

Why didn't he care? There was still so much he wanted to do in the time he had left on earth, and yet, he didn't really care if he did it anymore.

"This is it, Mac." The cab driver's voice brought him back to Los Angeles.

Bill paid him and stepped onto the sidewalk. He took in his surroundings: cracked and uneven sidewalks, crumbling old office buildings and warehouses, graffiti on every wall. *Ol' Bernie sure isn't wasting much money on high rent. My kind of neighborhood.*

He stepped through the painted wooden door with its boarded up glass window and walked into a plush office. The carpet was thick and luxurious and royal red. The furniture was modern, with mauve and grey color coordination, and there was a computer at all four of the desks in the entry office.

"May I help you?"

He looked at the sexy brunette behind the long grey receptionist counter. Her lipstick was too dark. "Yeah, I'm looking for Bernie."

She punched a button on her switchboard phone. "And who should I say is calling?"

"His cousin."

"Which cousin might that be?"

"His favorite cousin, who else?"

She spoke into the mouthpiece of the phone, smearing some of her lipstick on it. "Bernie, your favorite cousin is in the lobby." She paused. "I don't know if it's Marvin or not. He just said it was your favorite cousin. Yessir." She hung up the phone.

"He says to come right up. Are you Marvin?"

Bill smiled. "See? I told you he'd know who it was, didn't I?" He glanced for the stairs. "Where are the stairs?"

"Stairs? Why don't you take the elevator?"

Bill patted his chest. "Doctor says I should get more exercise."

"Five flights?"

Bill raised an eyebrow. "He said it would do me

good."

She shook her head. "You've got more willpower than me." She nodded to her right. "Behind that door."

Bill gave her a flirting wink and a wave as he opened the door and stepped into the stairwell. His heart thumped heavily in his chest as he slowly climbed the stairs, one step at a time. He didn't want to be exhausted when he faced Bernie.

On the fifth floor, he stepped into the hallway and searched the doors for an indication of Bernie's office. A middle-aged woman in a dark blue business suit stepped out of an office and approached him.

"Are you looking for someone, sir?"

"My uncle. Bernie. I haven't been here for a while, and I can't remember which office is his."

She smiled and softened the hard business-like look on her face. "It's right down there, at the end of the hall."

"Thanks. You've been very helpful. What is your name?"

"Mildred."

"Thank you, Mildred. I'll be sure and tell Uncle Bernie to give you a raise."

She smiled and waved him off. He turned and walked slowly to the large mahogany door with its opaque window at the end of the hall. He tried the door and found it unlocked. Quietly, he opened it and stepped inside.

A large, heavy-set man sat at an oversize executive desk, his back to the door, staring out the window at the slums below. He turned slowly and saw Bill standing to the side of his desk, only a few feet from his chair.

"Who are you?"

Bill picked up the old-fashioned brass letter opener on the desk and put it to Bernie's throat. "That's no way to talk to your star bounty hunter, Bernie."

"Rutledge?" His voice was two octaves higher than it had been only a moment before.

"None other. Now, you put your hands on your head and don't move, Bernie, old boy, or you're gonna make a big mess all over this nice clean office."

Bernie did as ordered. "What do you want?"

Bill rummaged through the desk until he found what he was looking for. He picked up the 9 mm Smith and Wesson semi-automatic and hefted it in his left hand. "Nice gun, Bernie. Expensive too. But I guess you can afford it from what I've seen." He pointed the gun to Bernie's head and cocked the hammer.

"What do you want?" screeched Bernie.

Bill pulled the gun from Bernie's head and sat on the edge of the desk. "I want a life for a life, Bernie, old buddy."

"What are you talking about?"

"You sold me out, Bernie. You gave Carrera my location for two hundred thousand dollars."

"You can have the money, all two hundred thousand of it -- in cash."

Bill's mind churned as he fought his scruples to kill this man and be done with it. "Two hundred thousand, Bernie? I thought I told you I've done this once before. You got two-hundred thousand from Carrera and you don't forfeit bond if the fugitive is dead. You owe me two-hundred thousand for bringing them back, and two-hundred thousand for the trouble you caused me and my parents."

"Are they dead?"

Bill thought he saw a look of glee in the big man's eyes. Before he realized what he was doing, he slapped him across the cheek with the barrel of the pistol. Bernie fell from his chair and onto the carpeted floor. He lay there, his hands covering his face, whimpering.

"To hell with the money, Bernie. I came here to kill you, you useless piece of shit. I might as well get it over with."

"No! Please!" He crossed his arms in front of his head.

"You're covering the wrong part of your anatomy, Bernie. I'm going to shoot you in the balls first -- providing you've got any. Then I'm gonna blow off your kneecaps. How does that sound?"

"You've gone crazy! You're out of your mind!"

"Yeah, I think you're right on that one, Bern."

"You'll never get out of here alive."

"Do you really think that kind of thing bothers a crazy man?"

"I swear to you. They promised you and your family no harm."

"Bern, Bern, you surprise me. What did you think I was going to do -- just hand them over without a fight?"

"I don't know. I swear, I didn't even think about it."

"That's because you don't give a damn, Bernie." He sat back on the desk. "I'm sure it will pain you no end to know that none other that Carrera himself went with his boys. And I'm sure you'll also find it painful to hear that he met his premature demise with them. Not all of them -- one of them is alive and well and told me all about your deal, Bern."

"I swear to God--"

"Ah ah." Bill waved the pistol at him. "Don't mention God, Bernie. Don't even think the word." Bill sat in the chair behind the desk while Bernie remained cowed on the floor. He picked up the phone and dialed Arizona information. When he had the number he wanted, he placed his call.

After several rings, a voice answered, "Benson Medical Center."

"I'm checking on the condition of my sister, Julie Short. She was admitted during the night for gunshot wounds."

"One moment please."

A familiar voice came on the line. "Bill, is that you?"

"Hi, Dad. How's Julie?"

"She's gonna be all right."

Bill's hand began to tremble. "What?"

"She's gonna be all right. The bullets missed all the vital organs. Her lungs are fine. No arteries damaged. She's already awake."

"Are you sure, Dad?"

"Of course I'm sure. Your mother and I've been here all the time. She's already asked for you."

"For me?" He felt a lightness in his chest. The phone weighed a ton. "How's Mike? Is he in jail?"

"He's fine. They took him to jail, but he's back at the hospital now. I guess they let him out to be with Julie. I don't know how they can do that kind of stuff, but he's standing right next to me. He wants to talk to you."

Bill looked down at Bernie's cowering figure. "Put

him on."

"Hello, Bill?"

"Is this Mike?"

"Yeah, this is Mike."

"You don't sound like Mike. What happened to 'man' and all that stuff?"

"Where are you?"

Bill kicked Bernie in the ribs. The big man moaned with pain. "You hear that? That's your friend and mine, the bondsman."

"What the hell are you doing there?"

"Hey, what is this -- an inquisition? I'm still running this show. Why aren't you in jail anyway? I find that unusual, even for Benson."

"Bill, come back to Tucson. Forget about that bondsman. Julie is being transferred to Saint Mary's Hospital in about two hours."

"He set us up, Mike."

"So what are you going to do -- kill him? For Christ sakes, get out of there and get back to Tucson. Julie wants to talk to you."

"She really is going to be all right?"

"One hundred percent. Now get out of there before you do something really stupid."

"I'll think it over, Mike." He hung up the phone and smiled down at Bernie. "You just got a reprieve, Bernie. Now what was it you were saying about that four-hundred thousand?"

The cab stopped in front of the lobby of Saint Mary's Hospital and Bill stepped into the warm desert air. He tipped the cabby ten dollars and rushed inside. After obtaining directions to the intensive care unit at the information counter, he fairly bounced down the hallway toward the west end of the building. So deep was he in his thoughts, he walked by his father without seeing him.

"Bill. Over here."

His father waved to him from the smoking area outside the large plate glass window, Mike at his side, a big grin on his face. Bill joined them and greeted each with a handshake. He put a cigarette between his lips and lit up.

"Where's mom?'

"She's in with Julie. They don't like too many people in the room at a time. Seems like your mom has been monopolizing most of the visiting time," answered Sam.

Bill glanced at Mike. "You wanna tell me how you got out of jail?"

"It's kind of a long story. I'll tell you all about it after you've seen Julie. I hate to get interrupted in the middle of a good story. You know what I mean?"

Bill nodded. "I can hardly wait."

Frona stepped into the smoking area and joined the men. Bill hugged her tightly and said, "How is she?"

""She's fine. They've got a bunch of tubes hooked to her, but most if it is monitoring equipment. They say she'll be out of intensive care in a day or so."

"Can I see her now?"

Frona nodded. "Lord, I wish you would. That's all that girl's been talking about since she came to. Get on in there and shut her up." She winked at Mike and Sam.

Bill was in the intensive care lobby and into the unit in a matter of seconds. Julie was in section nine, on the far west end of the wing. He approached her cautiously, afraid his mere presence might endanger her chances of survival.

She lay on her back, eyes closed. Even with the catheter in her nose, and her face drained of color, she looked beautiful to Bill. She opened her eyes slowly and fluttered her lashes to focus. A smiled beamed across her face and she lifted a hand weakly.

Bill stood at her bedside and took her hand into his. "How you feelin' there, Peaches?"

"Lousy." Her smile widened.

"Actually, you don't look so hot, now that you mention it."

The smile left her face. "I missed you, Bounty Hunter."

"You didn't think I'd leave you until you were delivered did you?"

"Mister macho man, huh?"

"What are you talking about?"

"You. That's what I'm talking about. What do you think I'm talking about?"

"Settle down. Don't get your blood pressure up. You're about to send the machine into the tilt mode."

She smiled again. "Why do you pretend you don't care about me?"

"Of course I care about you -- you and Mike both."

"I don't mean that way."

"You mean -- like boy friend-girl friend?"

She nodded slowly. "Like that."

"We've been over that ground, you little dingbat. I'm old enough to be your father."

"But you're not my father."

He squeezed her hand gently. "No. I guess I'm not."

"See? We're making headway."

"What headway?"

"You know I love you." She shook her head. "Damnit! There, you made me say it. I swore I wouldn't until you did. Damn."

"Until *I* did? What do you mean, you love me?"

She raised herself up a little on the bed. "Don't you know what that means, Bounty Hunter?"

"You can't even say my name."

"That was sure a fine piece of shooting in your folks' place. I never even saw your hand move. Next thing I knew, you were blasting the hell out of everything in the room."

"I owe you my life, Peaches. Thanks."

"So give it to me."

"What?"

"Your life."

"You talk like a sailor. I don't find that attractive in a woman."

"I'll go to church every Sunday and never utter another cuss word."

"You think I believe that?"

"Is that all that's holding you back?"

"Back from what?"

"From admitting how you feel. I know you feel it. I can feel you feeling it."

Bill felt the lump in his throat grow until he had to swallow. "Look...I uh...Why don't we uh...finish this conversation when you get out of here?"

"You're so close to admitting it. I think it's funny."

Bill released her hand and stepped back from the bed. He looked at her silently for several moments, then moved close, bent down and kissed her on the cheek. "Yeah, you're right. But don't you ever tell anybody else I said it."

"Said what?"

"You know. Do I have to say it?"

Her grin stretched from ear to ear. "Yes. I just want to hear it one time."

He took her hand in his and moved his face close to her. "I love you, Peaches. I swear I do. I don't know how something so stupid can happen, but it has. I've got some money now, and I'm going to see to it that you and Mike have the best attorney in the world. Once this thing is behind you, and you've had time to put some distance between what's happened and how things are in real life, I'd like to see you again."

"See me again?" Her breath was warm on his lips. "I'm talking forever, you idiot. Can't you see beyond the nose on your face."

"I'd rather not be one of those idiots, and I'd rather get all of this drug money and murder stuff out of the way, then, if you want to talk, we'll talk."

"Talk is cheap. We won't talk. We'll make love, and you'll hold me all night long. We'll wake up to the songs of birds and have breakfast together on the veranda."

"Veranda?"

"Bill, I don't have to get anything behind me. It's over. It's a really long story, but it's over."

"What are you talking about?"

"Mike and I got into trouble, but we cut a deal with

the DEA. Carerra was at the heart of it. I guess you delivered him for us, huh?"

Bill stepped back. "What? You mean you were trying to get Carerra to the DEA?"

"We couldn't tell you. We didn't know who you were. Besides, under the circumstances, you never would have believed us."

Bill sighed. "No wonder Mike got out of jail so fast." He looked down at her. "All of this time, you had me feeling sorry for you -- and my folks got involved."

"That shouldn't have happened. We didn't figure on the bondsman. Mike told me." Strength came to her eyes and she stared at him. "You were going to kill him, weren't you?"

"Who?"

"The bondsman."

"You think I'm gonna answer that question?"

"Bill, you're one of the strangest people I've ever known. That would have been an awful thing for me to live with."

"I thought you were dead."

"And that's why you were going to kill him?"

"A snitch." Bill turned his back to the bed and threw his hands in the air. "I don't believe it. A snitch."

"Bill."

He turned and faced her again. "You know, you may not be keeping score, but I am, and that's the third time in the last five minutes you've called me by my name."

"I love you, Bill Rutledge. I've never loved anything more. I'm sorry about Laura. She's a pretty woman, and she's a good person, and I know you think a lot of her, and I almost wrote you off because of her, but I can't. I love you too much. I want you for me. If that makes me selfish, then I'm selfish."

Bill shook his head. "Makes you human. I fought it as long as I could, Peaches -- right up to Bernie's office -- but I couldn't think of any other reason I could be driven to such an irrational act as killing a man in cold blood. And even then, I couldn't do it. I love you, Julie. I don't understand it, but I do. Maybe I'll come to my senses in time to be saved -- who knows?" He shot her a quick glance, a smile on his lips and in his eyes. "I have some weird habits, you know."

She smiled silently, her eyebrows arched.

"I'm not going to get rid of any of my cars."

She continued to stare at him.

"As a matter of fact, I'm going to look for a '69 GTO convertible tomorrow."

"With a four-speed transmission and a ram air four engine, right?"

"Of course."

Julie smiled and tried to sit up in the bed. "Can you kiss me around these tubes?"

A nurse came running to her bedside. "What are you doing, young lady? Your blood pressure is skyrocketing. You lay back in that bed right now, or I'll get restraints put on you."

"That won't be necessary, nurse. I just want a kiss from the man I love, then I'll go to sleep."

Bill moved next to the nurse and maneuvered his lips around the tubes in Julie's nose. He kissed her lips gently and brushed them with his tongue.

"Whoa, there, sir. Her blood pressure just went to

the critical level. I'm going to have to ask you to leave for now. You can take that up when she's feeling better."

    He smiled at the nurse as he backed out of the room. "That we will, ma'am. That we will."

The End

Made in the USA
Lexington, KY
14 March 2019